Rebel in Skorval

Katie Dunn

ISBN-13: 979-8-9852468-7-2

Facebook.com/AuthorKatieDunn/

Kdunnauthor.com

Titles by Katie Dunn

Ancient Elements

Myth Blessed

Four Horsemen

Sapphire Sparks

<u>Skor Stone Trilogy</u>
Pirates from Under
Prince of Shayd
Rebel in Skorval

Chapter 1

-Ana-

My name is Ana and I am a rebel

I stared down at my hand. It had been two days since I left the Shayd mines. Two days since I battled my uncle on the bridge. Two days since Kip… I squeezed my eyes shut and clenched my hand.

I wanted to chop my hand off.

It was useless.

It was not able to hold him.

I swung my fist out and connected with tree bark. The tree was unyielding, but the pain was instantaneous and intense. I cradled my injured hand to my chest as I hissed through the pain, but I deserved it. Not for the first time, I wanted to curl up in a ball and cry. However, now was not the time. My uncle had fled to Skorval where the Kings and Queen were being held. Against their will? No. They did not have will because my uncle drugged them with skor at his crowning ceremony in the Shayd capital. We must find him and free the monarchs of the other kingdoms then take our revenge.

If you asked me last week if I was going to kill my uncle in order to stop him, I would have said there had to be another way. Now, all I saw was red and rage fueled my desire to end my uncle for what he had done.

"You got something against trees now?" A familiar voice teased from behind me.

I turned to my best friend and saw the same heartache in his expression. Kip was Tlaren's brother in all ways except blood. He probably felt worse than all of us about Kip's death seeing as how he had helped my uncle find and fight us. My uncle at some point along our journey had drugged the Prince with skor. I believed it was at the coronation ceremony when Lord Sorden gave wine to all the royals. We found out the Lord of Skorval had a way to turn the skor into a powder form and had laced the local waters with it. We had to keep Ren tied up for a couple days but thankfully he was no longer under its influence.

Ren gave me a small smile and came over to inspect my hand that had fresh blood on the knuckles.

"I think Gesebe has some healing water with her."

I glanced to the makeshift camp we set up near the outskirts of Skorval. Gesebe had accompanied Jasta and some others from Under. They went directly to Skorval but when we did not show up in time they came to find us and our paths met along the way. They found us a day ago.

A day too late.

It was surprisingly nice to see the short Councilwoman. She was the only one who was nice to me when I was a captive in the underwater city of Under. She was also the one to give me the healing water that saved Kip from an arrow attack back in Drisl. She was the only member of the pirates/Council to stay in Under when we all started the mission, but it looked like she was done being left behind.

"I am fine," I said, instead of taking him up on the offer. My knuckles stung but it was nothing compared to the pain in my chest.

Ren drew closer and his voice dropped. I looked up at the change, but he was looking at the others of our party. "I know you do not want to hear this right now, but we must push forward. Everyone will be looking to you now."

He crossed his arms and finally turned back to me. Due to his sleeveless shirt, I was able to see the bright red zigzag tattoo stark against his darker islander skin indicating his Princely status. Soon, whenever we got his father back from Skorval, another zigzag would be added to his arm to show him moving from Prince to King. He was twenty-one now which was the age when the next ruler was supposed to take over.

If I did not hate my uncle and was not opened to the truth of his ways, then in two years' time I would have taken over for Lord Sorden as his heir. However, now I knew that even if I took over, he would still rule by controlling me with skor. He would not let a simple thing such as age stop him from ruling over all the kingdoms. He had been planning this for thirteen years. Prince Kipsien, as the rightful heir, was supposed to stop him but now it seemed it was up to me.

I nodded once then pressed my lips into a determined line before I walked over to the others. Jasta was the first to see me and she stood from her seat on a tree stump to greet me with a pat to my shoulder. I gave her a weak smile then turned to the others, Jasta and Ren at my back.

"Listen up."

Everyone's attention turned to me. I looked out over all the anxious faces. Ones I recognized as the Princes and Princess of the kingdoms and the Council from Under and ones I did not recognize but knew they came along on the journey from Under to help fight back. For days now we had only a handful of people on this mission but now we had more than enough, especially if we included Cailyn's village and the miners both of which were sent a letter yesterday and would meet us in Skorval as soon as they could.

"Lord Sorden will have guards and the elite warriors patrolling the city and the mountains looking for us. I would also not be surprised if guards from the other kingdoms are on their way to side with their Majesties. We have just about everyone in Skorval against us. They see us as traitors. As rebels. That means we will need to sneak in. A team will infiltrate the mines to look for Lord Sorden's secret alchemy lab and disrupt the skor production, another team will find places inside the palace to keep tabs on Their Majesties and the other people in the palace, and the last team will talk to the residents in the various rings to sort out alliances and work on ridding skor from the town."

I looked around our small gathering and pointed at Oskai and Jasta. "Oskai will lead the team to the palace." I raised my eyebrows at him. He confirmed my words with a nod. "Jasta will lead a team into the mines seeing as she is the only one of us to have seen the lab." I looked to Jasta for her approval, and she nodded as well.

"And you will be in charge of the town?" Jasta asked, picking up on my plan.

"I was thinking of putting Gesebe in charge of the town, but I will tag along and help out where I am needed. I know some people that we can trust, and the elite warriors live in the village. I am hoping to get them to side with us, especially after they saw our fight at the coronation and Shayd mines. They must be confused. I will be there to clear things up and they should trust me since I was, no, *I am*, their Saya."

I clapped my hands. "Now, choose which team you will side with and let us go."

It was not long until we were all divided and on our way into Skorval. Since Skorval was nestled in the three tallest mountains of Shayd, there were only three ways in. One way was from the sea but we were on the opposite side of the mountains to enter from that side. One way was through a series of winding trails and wooden platform lifts but those were heavily guarded, and we could be easily spotted. The other, which was the most dangerous, was to use the paths then climb the rest of the way around the mountain to the village. All the pirates had Hooks, courtesy of their resident inventor and Councilman of Under, Lenman. Besides me, that left the rest without a secure way up the mountain.

I led them up the trail until I spotted the first platform where the trail suddenly ended. I stopped before we reached it. Making a quick decision, I turned to the others.

"The Council, royals, and I will head this way, seeing as how we would be the most identifiable," I said pointing to the right of the path which led to craggy, sloped, mountain sides. "Cailyn will escort the rest of you up the trail and into Skorval safely. We will meet in the center of town near Granny's." At their confused looks I mentioned, "You will know it when you see it."

I looked to Cailyn, our Shayd bandit. She looked like she wanted to protest but pressed her lips into a thin line and nodded instead.

Cailyn waved her arm at her group, and they began their easy ascent up the mountain using the platforms to get to the next part of the trail and where the first guard would be.

I saw that Gesebe did not move and turned to her. "Gesebe you should probably go with them."

She frowned and turned to me. "I am part of the Council. I have a Hook and I am originally from Shayd."

I tilted my head in acknowledgement but shook my head. "That may be, but you do not have experience with this stuff." I said and gestured to the mountain. "You do not usually go on raids with the others and unless you climb underwater domes in your free time then I think you should go with them. Plus, as one of the Councilors of Under you can lead them."

She pursed her lips then looked toward the group slowly disappearing up the trail. I knew she agreed when she sighed.

"Fine, you're right." Then she turned and pointed a finger at me. She was much shorter than me, so she had to look up to glare at me. "But this is the last time I am being separated from you all." Then she stomped up the path to Cailyn and the others.

When I saw them reach the platform in the distance, we split off from them and started our treacherous climb.

Since the royals did not have Hooks, they were partnered with one of the pirates. I chuckled when I saw Prince Edsen and Princess Edrah outclimbing their partners. They lived in Drisl which was all in the trees, so they grew up climbing. Prince Tlaren seemed to be handling his climb well too. I would not be surprised if climbing was part of the training that his father, King Trost of Tripscari, put him through. The one I was worried about was Prince Shanm. He lived in the desert land of Farlo. There were not any trees or mountains to practice climbing in Farlo. Unless he liked to go around scaling the walls of his castle, which I doubted, then he needed help more than any of us.

I kept an eye on Prince Shanm as we free climbed up the mountain. We had to climb to the side instead of up in some places to avoid the paths, platforms, and guards that would be near both. About halfway up we found a ledge large enough for a small group of people and I called for a rest. Some of the pirates were breathing hard and Prince Shanm looked like he was about to collapse. My own arm muscles twinged since I had not climbed around these mountains in a few weeks.

Had it really only been a few weeks since I set out from these mountains and got kidnapped by pirates?

Water canteens were pulled out and I reminded everyone to save some for the rest of the climb before pulling my own out and taking a swig.

Ren sidled up next to me and looked up. "How much farther do you think is left until we start our descent?"

I looked up to gauge the distance. "I would say we are about halfway up. There will be less paths and guards up here so we may be able to walk some of it rather than climb the whole way." That was if Lord Sorden had not raised security since our attempted coup.

"Would using the Hooks be a good idea to get us the rest of the way up?" He crossed his arms and looked down at the device hooked to my waist.

I smirked and turned to my friend. "Are you tired already?"

He didn't hesitate to answer. "Yes."

I chuckled then glanced around at the other members of our climbing party until I found who I was looking for.

"Lenman, come here."

The tall Farloan made his way around the others, being careful not to knock anyone off the small ledge. His weapon of choice, a staff made from Drislian wood, was strapped to his back and poked out at his shoulder and leg. He wore an archer's hood despite not being an archer and had the hood drawn up around his bald head. When he reached us, his usual pleasant mood was subdued as it had been for two days.

"Do you think we could use the Hooks now?"

Lenman looked up the mountain and rested his hand on his belt where his Hook laid. He studied the rocks above for a moment then nodded. "We can use them now but you will have to guide us around the paths so the guards do not see the lines and we will have to move a bit slower to make sure each line is secure."

"Of course. The paths curve to the left from here so as long as we stick to the right, we should be able to make it up and around before we have to descend into the village."

I turned to the others and relayed our plans which meant the royals had to stick with their partners now. Prince Shanm would go with Lenman. Princess Edrah would go with Jasta. Prince Edsen with Oskai and Prince Tlaren with me.

Lenman and Shanm were the first to go. I pointed to an area to the right that should be out of view of the guards, and he shot the Hook. It latched on to a rock and he pulled at his end of the line to make sure it was secure then saluted us as he pressed the button in his hand, and they were whisked away.

The rest of us followed and we continued doing it the rest of the way up. I found it was both harder and easier to get up the mountain that way. On the one hand, we were speeding up faster than the paths and platforms would have been but on the other hand, it was terrifying to free hang there while I disconnected the Hook from the rock so I could shoot it again.

The higher we went, the more the wind battered us and made our journey more precarious. The cold started to seep in though it was still day and the sun helped fight off the chill, though only slightly. It was a blessing that there was no snow otherwise that would have made our journey impossible.

At the top of the mountain, we took another rest. I knew the paths and platforms would be descending from there, so all we needed to do was take them down since the checks by guards had already been done and the rest would not care as much to look too closely at the newcomers. I closed my eyes and breathed in the air. It was so fresh and crisp up there. At that point, we could see the other two peaks of the mountains that surrounded Skorval. On one of them I could just make out a green and gold structure that I recognized as the palace. My home.

The sight of it sent both an ache of longing and a heat of anger and betrayal through me. I wanted to forget the plan and just march into the palace and confront my uncle. My fingers twitched, wanting to reach for my swords despite being on a separate mountain from the man. As if reading my intentions,

Ren gripped my arm and pursed his lips as if to hold me back, but his eyes promised *soon.*

Letting out a calming breath, I waved everyone forward and we all put away our Hooks before starting our trek down the mountain to meet with our other group and complete our missions. As we took the first steps, a frightened shout rang out and rocks skittered down the mountain. I turned in time to see the dark curly hair, ruby earring, and terrified expression of Prince Shanm before he disappeared down the mountainside.

Chapter 2

-Kip-

"Kip, stay with me!"

I squeezed my eyes closed more than they already were as Ana's voice echoed, no, it thundered, through my head. When the voice drifted away, I relaxed again and drifted back to sleep.

"No! Kip, stay with me!"

Why was Ana shouting? 'Just let me sleep' I told her, but my mouth did not move. In fact, my whole body could not move. I tried to lift my arm, but something was restraining it. My mind suddenly woke up as a flood of panic hit me. I tried to open my eyes, but they would not move either.

'Ana! Ana, help!'

"Kip, stay with me!"

Her voice sounded far away and it took me a moment to realize that I did not hear her physically but rather I was remembering her panicked voice saying those words. But why would she think I would be leaving her?

Instead of trying to move all parts of my body, I focused on one thing. The effort was draining but eventually I felt my pinkie finger move. Relief, albeit a tiny amount, replaced a bit of the panic. I tried again and this time felt two fingers move. Alright, now to try to open my eyes.

My eyelids were annoyingly heavy, and it took more effort than a couple of fingers to open them even for even a second. Bright light hit my retinas and I squeezed my eyes shut again. Not that I had to force them shut, the heaviness did that for me. I tried again.

This time I blinked a couple times to adjust to the light and was able to keep them open. Fogginess pulled at my mind, wanting me to go back to sleep. I ignored the feeling and looked around. My head still would not move so I could only see a little in the position I was in. A pointed ceiling with rafters were above and a window which was the source of the bright light was on the wall in front of me. A small table sat next to me with a bloodied washcloth hanging over a basin of what I assumed to be water. I was not going to get much farther with sight, so I used my other senses to try and figure out where I was. I could not move but I could feel the soft mattress below me and something like cloth covering my body. A blanket perhaps? My jacket and hat were not on so someone must have taken them off before putting me in bed. But whose bed? I sniffed the air but did not pick up anything that would give me a hint of where I was. Only the sounds of insects buzzing outside could be heard which did not indicate anything either.

How did I end up there?

"Hello?" I called out, this time my mouth moving enough for me to be able to let out sound though my voice came out soft and croaked as if I had not used it in a while. I tried again, this time a little louder. "Hello?"

A door creaked open to my left, but I could not see who came in. A moment later an older woman's face appeared above me.

"You're awake?" She asked.

I figured it was a rhetorical question since she could obviously see I was awake. "Where am I?" I croaked.

She ignored my question and shouted behind her to someone out of my sight. "Gino! Come here! He is awake!"

I heard footsteps pound down a hallway and an older man about the same age as the woman appeared beside the lady and looked down at me with wide eyes. "Well, I'll be." He patted the woman on the back and smiled fondly at her. "Well done, dear. You saved him."

Saved me? From what? And I still could not move!

"It was touch and go there for a bit, but he pulled through." The woman looked down at me proudly.

"What is going on?" I said softly. My eyelids started to droop but I fought the drowsiness. I needed answers. I needed my friends.

The woman tucked the cover around me more tightly even though it was unnecessary. "Sleep now. I will answer all your questions and have food for you when you awaken."

I tried to nod but my head stayed paralyzed. I let my eyelids fall shut and the darkness took me into a dreamless sleep.

The next time I awoke, the sunlight coming through the window was not as bright. I tested out my movement with my fingers and found they were still restricted by a covering, but I could move them underneath. I tested out my head next and was able to turn it side to side to take in the rest of the room that I could not see before. The door on my left was cracked open and there in a chair in the shadowed corner laid my coat, hat, and sword.

I attempted to sit up but the blanket that was tightly wrapped around me struggled for dominance. The effort to sit up wore me out faster than I would have liked but I continued until I won and was able to push the covers back and sit up. A smell caught my attention and I looked to the right to find the bloody washbasin gone and in its place a tray of bread and cheese with a cup of what looked to be tea. I reached for the tea and took a sip and almost spit it out. The tea had gone cold and tasted a bit like dirt but my throat screamed at me for liquid so I threw back the rest and swallowed it before my tastebuds could argue. Next, I crammed the bread and cheese into my mouth and almost moaned at how fresh it was. Since the tea had gone cold, I would assume the tray had been there for more than a couple hours which meant the lady of the house expected me to wake soon.

I shifted so I could get out of the bed then walked stiffly over to the chair and put my things back on. My body was sore all over and I could not remember what caused it. Maybe the lady would know.

I walked over to the crack in the door and peeked out. A couch and rug faced me and beyond that was what looked to be the kitchen. No one else in sight though. I crept out of the room and made sure to look around each corner before moving beyond it. I stopped at a window and peered outside to see a forest of tall, needled trees on land that sloped upward. So, I was still in Shayd then. Specifically, the area near the mountains in the north of Shayd. How did I get there and where was my crew? A door next to the window made me realize I could just leave now before anyone noticed. I could go find a town then search for my friends.

I reached for the door handle but a woman's voice behind me made me freeze.

"I wouldn't do that if I were you."

I immediately reached for my sword but paused before pulling it out. She was not an enemy. If she wanted me dead, she would not have saved me. Saved me from what though, I was still unsure. I slowly turned around and assessed the woman. Her graying hair was pulled into a bun and she held a metal ladle in one hand. I could tell that it was more than just a cooking utensil. If she wanted to, she could probably do some damage with that thing.

I nodded at the ladle then looked her in her gray-green eyes. "Do you plan on stopping me?"

She looked down at her cooking utensil then burst out laughing. "Oh, this?" She raised it up and I stiffened which only made her laugh harder. "Dearie, I am only making soup. Even in your weakened state I do not think I could prevent you from leaving if you were determined to. However, I do not think it is wise to leave yet." Her laughter disappeared and a look of pity entered her eyes as her lips pressed together. "You had quite an accident."

Accident. That word sent a shiver of panic through me. Was my crew okay? The royals? Ana?

"Accident?" I asked softly, feeling a weight pressing down on me. I did not think I could handle it if she said I was the only survivor of a tragic accident involving my friends.

She lifted her ladle again and waved it in the air. "I do not know what exactly happened but one day I was out strolling along the small river nearby and I found you laying there, bloodied, unconscious, and on the verge of death."

I blinked as the story brought memories to mind. A battle. A fall and a desperate grab. Beautiful green eyes full of unshed tears peering down and pleading for me not to let go.

I gasped and clutched my chest.

Oh, Ana. She must think me dead.

I spun around and marched to the door. "I must go find my crew."

Just as I reached for the handle, the door opened, and a cheery older man walked in carrying a pile of chopped wood. The name Gino flitted through my mind.

"Oh!" The man stumbled back, startled. Then a huge grin greeted me. "Good to see you up and about, lad."

Gino's gaze flitted to his wife and silent communication passed between the two before he focused on me again.

"Have you had some of my wife's soup? It can cure just about anything." The man chuckled as he moved around me to set the wood near the entrance to the kitchen.

The woman came closer and laid a hand on my shoulder, her eyes full of care and sympathy. "Rest awhile longer and let me look at your wounds before you go."

Glancing towards the door, I debated my options. I did not know how long it had been since the battle with Lord Sorden, but my crew might have already moved on to complete the mission. I knew it was what I would have wanted. Which means they are in Skorval or on their way to it and that would be at least a day or two trek from this house I would expect, assuming I was near the mines. I could move and walk around but I could not deny that the fatigue and soreness in my muscles and whatever else was still plaguing me would hinder my journey.

I nodded and turned back to the kind lady and let her guide me to a seat at a small wooden table meant for two. A while later, a bowl of soup was placed in front of me and the woman sat in the vacant chair across from me. The man had gone to the back a while ago, presumably to his room, after lighting a fire in the fireplace using the chopped wood and had not appeared since.

"Now that you're awake, dearie, maybe you can answer a few things?" Although it was said as a question, she did not wait for an answer before asking her questions. "Do you remember anything? Your name? What happened? Where you are?"

I studied the woman's earnest face. She looked like she truly wanted to help but if I told her who I was, would she turn on me? I had no idea how far Lord Sorden's control went with the people of Shayd. Until I was stronger, I figured I should be vague about who I was.

"Folks call me Captain. I was headed to Skorval when I got into a bit of a skirmish on a bridge then…" I mime falling off the bridge with two fingers and the table as the cliff.

The woman nodded. "From the mines then, are you? That bridge has always been a bit unsteady. We get items raining down here occasionally. Never a person though, that one is new. You must be careful up there. It is a dangerous place."

My brows rose. "So, we are near the mines then?"

She nodded. "Oh yes, just a quarter mile that way," she said pointing to the left of her house, "and up the mountain."

That confirmation lifted some of the anxiety I had since awakening. "I need to get back up there."

She pursed her lips and looked out of her kitchen window. She was quiet, thinking, for a moment then she looked back at me and nodded towards the soup in my bowl. "Eat that up and stay one more night so I can make sure you are ready to travel then I will personally take you to the path that leads up to the mines in the morning."

I hesitated. I was ready to move out now despite the soreness in my body.

Seeing my hesitation, the woman held up one finger. "One night."

I deflated and gave her a nod. I could stay one more night. My body probably needed the rest. I only hoped the others were faring well.

Chapter 3

-Ana-

$\mathcal{M}$y heart stopped for a moment and my breath faltered. Shouts of denial rang around me as everyone surged to the edge to peer down, but I did not move.

No. This could not be happening again.

What would I tell King Domen once we rescued the Kings and Queen? What would Queen Rala say? She knew it was a dangerous mission and that was why she stayed home with the twins. Would Jiko or Jaija become the new heir? How would I tell Cailyn? She acted as if she did not care for the Prince's flirtations and advances, but I could tell he had been growing on her.

All those thoughts flitted through my mind in a tornado of panic while I stood frozen at the top of the mountain.

Then, words of hope penetrated my panic.

"Do not let go, we are coming to get you!" Ren shouted.

My head snapped to where the Prince was on the edge of the mountain. I rushed over, pushing my way through the crowd but being careful not to knock anyone down to join Prince Shanm. I peered down at what everyone was looking at and gasped with relief.

Prince Shanm must have grasped some rocks on the way down in a desperate grab and luckily caught onto a strong enough one that held him suspended in the air. He had not fallen to his death after all. His fingers were bloody from his previous attempts at grabbing at rocks and his forehead was shiny with sweat. He stared up at us with frightened eyes and risked a glance down before jerking his gaze back up with a terrified squeak. His fingers began to slide, the blood causing his hold to be slippery.

I immediately jumped into action.

I pulled the Hook from my belt and shot it at the ground. It struck the rough dirt and rocks and held tight, but I was unsure if it would stay there once I put weight on it. I looked up and met Lenman's eyes with a question in my own. He nodded in answer and I, hoping he was right, leapt off the mountain.

I started plummeting but thankfully I was jerked to a stop by the Hook. I let out a breath of air at the sudden stop and waited until I ceased spinning before looking around for Shanm. He was only a few feet away hanging on for dear life. He turned his head to look for me making the red ruby in his earring glimmer as it caught the light. He stared at me with hope and fear in his eyes.

"Hang in there, Shanm, I will be right there." I nodded and tried to put confidence in my tone to help calm him.

He adjusted his grip on the stone and I wondered how many times he had needed to do that. Probably more often now that the blood on his fingertips was causing his hold to loosen.

"Hurry," he gasped out.

I pressed my feet against the side of the cliff and bounced my way over to him. The height should have scared me, but I was used to rock climbing since my rooms in the palace were at the top of a mountain and the fastest way down to the docks was by climbing down rather than taking the paths.

When I was directly next to him, I adjusted the grip on the Hook and sent a silent prayer to the sky.

"Ok, Shanm, I am right here. What you are going to do is let go of one hand and lay it on my left shoulder. I am going to maneuver my way beneath you and when I am in position you will drop onto my back and curl your legs around me. Got it?"

"Ah you suh dis wi' work? I do not know ef I can hode on wif one hand dat long." His Farloan accent mixed with his fear made his words almost unintelligible, but I got the idea.

"You must hold on," I said, "and it *will* work." I could only hope.

"Hand on one, move on two, drop on three. Ready?" I did not wait for an answer.

"One!" I shouted.

He moved his left hand from the rock and placed it on my left shoulder. My body dipped with the weight but thankfully the line held.

"Two!"

He shifted right enough to let me in, and I positioned my body in front of him. I tried to be quick knowing his grip would fail at any moment.

"Three!" He dropped and his other hand landed on my other shoulder as his body curled around me from behind. I grunted at the new weight.

I gripped the Hook tighter and pressed the button that would bring us back up. We slowly rose as I spoke calm words to the panicked Prince. The boots of the others came into view and my forehead peaked over the top. Then we suddenly dipped and I was facing the rocks again. Shanm let out a terrified squeak and I gasped, trying not to panic.

"What is going on?" I shouted up to the others.

"Your line is detaching," Lenman called down calmly.

I pushed the button and we rose for a second before dipping again. It seemed shooting the end into the ground was not sturdy enough after all.

"Quick, pull them up," Lenman told the others.

They must have all teamed up because a second later we rose back up until I could see over the edge again. I could only imagine the strength needed to pull two full grown people up on one line. When we were close enough, strong, dark arms reached down and lifted the Prince off my back leaving me on the Hook's line. Then the same arms reached down for me and Lenman pulled me up. Shanm and I laid next to each other on the mountain top breathing in deeply and thanking the stars and sea for our lives. More accurately, we needed to thank Lenman and the others.

I lifted my head and flapped my hand at the group in an attempted wave. "Thanks everyone," I gasped out.

"Let me wrap your fingers," Jasta said and knelt next to Shanm.

He nodded and held out his hands to her while giving her a thankful smile. She pulled some bandages out of her bag and took care to wrap his fingers so they could heal. Lenman came over, blocking out the sun, and held out a hand to me. I took it and he pulled me up.

I patted my Hook. "Lenman, you should be a rich man. That invention of yours saves lives. Emergency crews could use it for situations just like that one."

He looked down at his shoes with a solemn expression. "It didn't save everyone and as we saw today it has flaws."

"Not everything is perfect the first go around. Now you know what to improve and when everything is settled, we can set up a shop for you...if you are interested. As for Kip, it could only save him if he was using it so do not give yourself a hard time about it." The pain in my voice was hard to hide but no one should be blaming Lenman or his Hook since no one thought to use it in the moment. That was on me, not him or his invention.

He took a deep breath and forcibly changed the subject. "So, should we move on then?" He stared down at the village far below, only a bunch of small dots from this far.

I nodded and turned to the others. "Now if we are all done with our break," I gave a small smile to Shanm to let him know I was jesting, "let us move on. The sooner we get to our positions the sooner we can bring the false King down."

They heartily agreed and we took the paths and platforms the rest of the way down. Many of us were relieved to be rid of the climbing and dangers of the rocky mountain. There were guards stationed along the paths and at the platforms occasionally but just as I suspected, they did not pay much attention to the goings of travelers, assuming the guards on the other side checked everyone thoroughly.

The closer we got, the bigger the village seemed. Up on the top of the mountain the town seemed tiny but now it stretched across the whole valley. Fields of crops and ranch houses made up the outer ring of the town then the closer we got to the center the less spaced the buildings became and more storefronts and stalls popped up. I noticed something new had been added to every street corner and it made me sad. The Skorval crest of three mountains with laurels on either side and three stars below shown on various flags but with an added crown symbolizing Lord Sorden's new reign as King. At the coronation, he had announced that design would be the official crest of Shayd, forgoing the traditional compass crest.

I led the others through the center of town, the smells from the vendors and calls of the street kids hitting me deep. I itched to put on my red coat, the symbol of my status in Skorval, but I knew that would draw too much attention. I was already risking being seen by not disguising my hair, face, or even scar.

Near Granny's, a café and bakery loved by all in the village, I slowed and told the others to keep an eye out for Cailyn or anyone else on their teams. It did not take long before I saw a flash of red hair through a window in Granny's. I poked my head through the door and looked around for the red and spotted Cailyn and the others sitting at the tables or milling about the place holding various drinks and baked goods. I turned to my group and told them to wait outside since the shop inside was full and went in to let Cailyn know we were there.

She spotted me, a hint of relief in her eyes, and stood to greet me. "I'm glad you made it. How are the others?" She whispered.

"They are outside, all fine."

Shanm could tell her what happened to him if he wanted the story to be shared, but knowing him, I did not think he would appreciate me scaring her with the tale and making him look bad in the process.

"Everyone on your end make it okay? Where is Gesebe?" I asked just now realizing the short Councilwoman was not present in my visual sweep of the bakery/café.

Cailyn waved toward the door. "She went to find items that would help disguise you all when you came back. She was not convinced the royals would get away with being unnoticed. Some of them have a big presence." She said the last part with goofy grin aimed toward the door as if she could see them from where we stood. More accurately, see *him.*

I rolled my eyes but had to admit Gesebe's idea was a good one. Ren's tattoo and Edrah's makeup along with her and Edsen's Drislian hair would be noticeable and they could be instantly identified by those characteristics.

"Alright, let us split into our groups and have team leaders go over their plans. Then once Gesebe is back and all necessary members are disguised we can split up."

Cailyn nodded and jumped into her role of leader by gathering everyone together and relaying the information. I brought the rest of the group inside, making the already full building cramped but Granny, as everyone called her, did not mind or suspect our true motivations. All she saw were customers and more money. Thankfully there were so many people that she did not recognize me among the crowd. I did not venture into the village very often when I was Saya but on the rare occasion I did go I always made sure to stop by this place and grab an apple tart and hot chocolate. Even now, among the preparations for our mission, I could not resist once I had a moment to breathe in the mouthwatering aromas. I sent Jasta and Lenman to get some treats and drinks for the pirates and royals while I gathered my group to talk business.

"Alright, remember what we discussed before. This group will be staying in the village to analyze the waters and suss out allies and skor. If anyone is not wanting to be a part of these things now is your chance to switch groups." I looked among the faces before me, some familiar and others strangers we picked up along the way, and waited.

No one moved and I felt a surge of pride in my chest. These were determined, motivated, and spirited individuals. They all had something to fight for and hopefully would help me find others who wanted our kingdom to change. The hard part would be convincing them about Lord Sorden and the skor and not setting off alarms in the process.

Lenman came back and handed out treats and drinks to those who had not gotten any yet. I clasped my hands around my cup of hot chocolate and let the warmth seep into my hands. I breathed in the sweet-smelling steam coming from the mug then took a tentative sip. I closed my eyes and sighed.

"That is the stuff," I said happily.

When I opened my eyes, the others were smiling at my reaction. Prince Shanm, who was careful not to hurt his injured hands further, hesitantly tried his own then his eyes widened in surprise. I supposed he never tried hot chocolate before or at least had not had any for a while since hot drinks were not popular in his kingdom due to the scorching weather. He nodded his approval and turned to Cailyn next to him, offering her his drink to try. She laughed and waved him away and held up her own cup that she was still drinking from before we arrived. It was nice to see Cailyn relaxed and smiling. A big difference from a few days ago.

I kept sipping my drink and taking bites of my tart as I divided the group into partners. Each set was tasked with a different section of the town anywhere from the outer rings to the center and would have four days to complete their missions. That gave us enough time to gather people as well as the other groups to infiltrate the mines and palace and set up things there.

I was the last one to be assigned since I would be moving among the groups, and it seemed I would be starting in town with Gesebe. Shanm and Cailyn of course partnered, and I could only hope they focused on their mission rather than flirting the whole time. However, knowing Cailyn for the brief amount of time I had, she would keep Prince Shanm in order.

I broke up the group and let them mill about while I checked on the others. Across the room was Ren, Lenman and Jasta with their group that would be heading into the mines and near the back of the café/bakery was Edrah, Edsen, and Oskai leading the group that would infiltrate the palace. Oskai wanted to stick with me seeing as how that was what Kip would have wanted but I convinced him that the palace was the most dangerous place to be and Edrah and Edsen would need him. He had grumbled but agreed. They got their plan laid out and partners divided up and now all we needed was Gesebe.

Just as I had the thought, Gesebe walked in grinning and holding up three large cloth bags bursting with various items. We cleared a table for her in the back, obscured by a wall on two sides and our bodies on the other two sides. Gesebe laid everything out and called the royals over. It was decided that the pirates and others in our rebel group did not need disguises since no one knew them. Even after the attempted coup during the coronation, no one remembered their features enough to make wanted posters.

Gesebe went to work on Edrah first. She washed off her purple and green eye makeup and handed her a hooded shirt that would cover her ultra-light blonde hair that was obviously of Drislian origin. When it was all done, Edrah looked like any other Skorval citizen. Edsen also had to cover his white-blond hair and was given a similar hooded shirt but bigger and baggier, and he had to take off his signet ring. His signet ring used to have a skor stone in the center but now held fluorite—a stone of purple and green. Shanm was deemed good to go except for his shirt which had too much color and patterns to be from Skorval. Lastly was Ren who only needed a long-sleeved shirt to cover his red zigzag tattoo. If anyone knew them personally, they would still be identifiable but to the common person they had no obvious royal markers.

I expected that to be the end, but Gesebe turned to me with a jar of cream the color of my skin.

"We should probably cover your scar," she said and eyed the small mark near my chin.

I wanted to protest and say my scar was not an identifying mark, but I knew it to be false, so I kept my mouth shut and accepted her small disguise. Once she put the cream on my chin, she moved around to the back of me and started unbraiding my hair. I moved out of her reach and yanked my hair around to hold tightly.

"Is that necessary?"

Gesebe put her hands on her hips. "Yes, it is all part of the disguise. You know, technically, you are a royal now."

That sent a pang of loss and unease through me. After all of this was over, I would become the Queen of Shayd—that is if the people accepted me.

"Alright, but I can do it myself."

Gesebe held up her hands as if saying *go for it.* I quickly unbraided my hair and let the wavy black locks tumble down my back. When I turned to her, she nodded her approval and packed up the rest of her materials.

Not to bring attention to us more than was already on us, I gathered the captains of the three groups and wished them success in their missions before sending them off. I hoped the next time we met, we would be standing in the Great Hall victorious.

We shuffled out of Granny's as the old woman waved at us and asked us to come again soon, completely oblivious that a rebel group had planned a coup right in her place of business. Ren and his group went northwest, headed for the mountain with the skor mines. As he passed, he placed his hand on my shoulder and whispered, "good luck."

Edrah's group left next going east toward the mountain that held my home. We hugged and I whispered in her ear how to access my rooms from the outside in case they needed it. She nodded letting me know she understood then led her group away.

We were the last and did not have a specific direction to go since we were already in the midst of the village. I sent the pairs off to their designated areas then turned to Gesebe to fill her in on what she missed. However, as I opened my mouth to speak, a voice spoke right behind me and a sharp point pressed into my back.

"Thought I wouldn't find out you were in town?"

So much for the disguise.

Chapter 4

-Kip-

As promised, the woman led the way to the path that would lead me to the mines the next morning. She had checked over me to make sure I was healed enough to make the journey then handed me my things. Gino stood by her side with a sack of food and medicine with firm instructions on how much to take and when. Both were only enough for a day so Gino suggested I stop for more when I got a chance.

After shrugging on my coat and placing my hat on my head the woman handed me something.

"This was in your hand when we first found you," she said.

I looked down and saw the Hook Lenman invented being held out to me. I slowly reached out and took it from her. When my fingers touched it, a memory flashed in my mind.

I had just let go of Ana's fingers and was plummeting to my death when I remembered something that I had forgotten when Princess Edrah and I had been in the hole—The Hook that my crew and I used to board ships and escape. With my heart thundering and time seeming to slow, I pulled it out of my belt and desperately aimed in a random direction. I pressed the trigger and the rope with the arrowed tip flew away then my body jolted to a stop. I halted in midair but ended up swinging into the side of the ravine which dislodged the Hook's hold on the rocks, and I tumbled the rest of the way down.

The Hook was probably what saved me. I was still badly injured, but it could have been worse.

The walk to the path was not too far but after a while my ribs began to ache anyway. My breaths came shallowly as I tried to withstand the pain and keep up with the old woman who seemed to have a quick step. Or maybe I was just unusually slow.

The river to the right of us was slow and thin yet it still gave off a refreshing smell and breeze. After a while, the woman stopped, and I held in a sigh of relief as I stopped next to her. I looked around but did not see any trail. The water had thinned though, probably only ankle deep now.

"This is it?" I asked, unbelievingly.

"Yes, sir. Just cross this river, pass through those trees, and there will be little stone markers that point you the rest of the way."

I nodded. "Ok, thank you...uh, I am sorry, but what is your name?" I only now realized I never caught her name despite talking to her for a day and her taking care of me.

She smiled wide. "It's Beatrice."

"Well, thank you, Beatrice. I will find you again and repay you. I am in your debt."

She waved my words away. "No, no dear, no need for that. I wasn't going to just let you die on the riverbank. Now go before it gets too late."

I nodded even though it was still morning, and a late day was not an issue. I headed toward the shallow river preparing myself to have cold, wet boots for the rest of the morning.

"Oh, Your Highness, do not forget this," Beatrice called out.

I turned before her words registered.

Her smile was sly as if I just confirmed her suspicions. She stepped towards me holding something out. It caught the light and glinted. It was my signet ring.

"I found this on you when I was dressing your wounds. I wondered if you were a thief but then I saw your tattoo."

I laid a hand over my arm where the tattoo was inked despite it being covered already by my coat. "Why did you not tell me before, or report me?"

"I remember when your parents were alive. Everyone was happy. Our kingdom prospered. It was such a shame when they died."

I looked at her warily. What she said was a sentiment held by many but that did not mean she did not like Lord—well, King now—Sorden or that she was not being manipulated by him.

"That does not answer my question," I said.

"I did not tell you about my suspicions before because it was your secret to keep. I did not report you because I have heard rumors about a pirate claiming to be the lost Prince trying to take back his kingdom from Lord Sorden. I did not believe the rumors but once I saw your signet ring and tattoo, I hoped it was true. Please, Your Highness," she stepped closer and clasped her hands, "take the throne and bring us back to our former glory and happiness."

I only had one last thing to ask. "You do not think King Sorden can do that?"

She scoffed. "We have lived down here for over a decade, and in that time, I have watched the Shayd mines get nearly replaced by the Skor mines and not enough resources given to the workers who stay up there. I have watched as people continue to lose their livelihoods and the capital to stay in ruins as well as every attempted monarch assassinated or mysteriously die. It is suspicious that Lord Sorden is the only one to survive into kinghood."

I raised my brows at the older woman. All of that and she did not mention the skor manipulation. I thought everyone was starry eyed over the new King because of his skor business helping the economy but it seemed some people, such as Beatrice and the people in Cailyn's village, saw past that to what was really happening.

Good. We needed all the allies we could get.

I bowed my head. "I will do my best." I turned to leave but remembered something. I looked over my shoulder at her. "How do you get your water?"

She furrowed her brows and looked toward the river.

I glanced at the moving water and back at her. "Do not drink any shared water, continue to use the river. Lord Sorden is…tainting the waters."

Her lips pressed into a grim line and she nodded once before beginning her trek back to her house and husband.

I placed my ring, which was on a cord, around my neck and started across the river. Past the trees, just as Beatrice said, I found a marker of stacked stones pointing through the woods to another marker I could barely make out from there. I continued on, following the stones all the way up the mountain. As the mountain began to become steep my breaths came faster, and I had to take frequent breaks. My ribs ached and my legs threatened to give out. I went to take a drink from my borrowed canteen and only a drop fell to my tongue.

I held in my groan and looked up to try to gauge where the sun's position was in the sky. I could not be certain, but it looked like it was directly overhead, meaning it was close to midday and I had been walking for hours. I knew the river began at the top which was where Cailyn's father had drunk from during his time at the Shayd mines but I had no idea how much longer until I would be there.

No way but forward.

I kept going for what felt like another half hour before the ground became level again and the trees started to disappear. I could see down the mountain now and off to my left was the bridge that had nearly ended my life. I shuddered and hurried to the entrance to the trail.

I had a moment of confusion when I came into the clearing. No one was around and I could not see the entrances to the mines from there. Had Beatrice sent me to the other side of the bridge?

No, I could see white tents off in the distance which meant I was near the miners' campsite. I ventured across the clearing and could finally see the entrance to the West mine. From there I was able to find my way to the river, well more of a stream, and fill my canteen. Once I got my fill, I checked some of the tents and the inside of the mines but there was no one around.

Weird. I would have guessed after a few days that the miners would be back at work.

I knew there was a town nearby. I could stay there for the rest of the day before starting my journey to Skorval and ask around about the miners. Maybe someone would even know about my crew.

Only one problem though.

I would have to cross the bridge.

I made my way over to it and stared at it a long time before I finally worked up the courage to move.

One step at a time, I could do it.

I placed one foot on the bridge, then another. Slowly I inched across as I gripped the ropes on either side. A sudden wind swept across the ravine, making the bridge sway. I froze, as panic flooded my body. The bottom of my long blue coat flapped around my legs and my tri-pointed hat was nearly torn from my head. I stayed in that position long after the wind died down until the bridge was settled once more.

I looked behind me and nearly groaned. I had only gone a few feet. I still had many more to go.

I was suddenly grateful the miners had not returned so that there were no witnesses to my cowardice.

What would be the best way to get across without freezing every few feet?

Too bad Lenman was not there to give me a device that could…I do not know, maybe fly me across or push me forward.

I inched along a bit more and breathed deeply as I did. I kept my gaze on the land at the end and chanted *almost there* to myself in my mind.

Another gust of wind had me crouching, nearly rolled into a ball, as the bridge swayed.

This was not working.

I closed my eyes and sucked in a breath through my nose and slowly released it through my mouth. I pictured Ana and the others beckoning me across the ravine to them. Their hopeful and encouraging expressions giving me strength. I stood straighter and released the rope. My heart beat harder and faster as my mind tried telling me I would fall if I did not hold onto the rope, but I forced myself to imagine land underneath my feet. I kept my eyes closed and started walking.

"I am on land. My friends are waiting for me over there. I am on land. My friends are waiting for me over there." Over and over I whispered it, using it as my motivational mantra, until my foot hit something hard and I stumbled.

I was certain I was going to fall off the bridge once again as my eyes flew open. My hands reached out to grab something, anything, but hit air. Then my mind caught up to what I was seeing and the panic drifted away.

A laugh burst from me and I spun to look at the way I came. I made it. My racing heart slowed to a normal pace and I faced the road that would lead me to my friends…and possibly my destiny.

Chapter 5

-Ana-

"Shula. Good to see my training has not failed."

I had expected the elite women warriors to be in the palace protecting all the royals. So why was Shula in the village? She was not among those who accompanied my uncle to the mines that fateful day so the last I had seen her was at the coronation.

Gesebe stood off to the side with wide eyes that flitted between me and the warrior. Gesebe slowly reached for something at her side. A dagger or a potion, I was not sure, but I knew Shula would kill her before the Councilwoman could fully pull it out. I shook my head slightly and Gesebe froze. Her brows dipped into a frown showing her disagreement, but I shook my head again. She pursed her lips but did as I suggested and did not pull out a weapon on the elite warrior.

"So, what brings you down to the village?" I asked casually.

"None of your concern…*Saya,*" She said in a tone that suggested I was a disgrace to the title.

I winced. Saya was a position held in the highest regard. It was the third most important position in Skorval after the Lord of the region and his heir which also happened to be me. Being Saya was dear to me and to insinuate that I was not a fit for the position hurt.

I tried to turn around to face her, but she pressed the blade into my back a bit harder. "Walk. Your friend too."

"Shula, you do not know what is going on. There is more at work here than he has told you." I did as she told and walked forward, clasping Gesebe's arm on the way and dragging her beside me. I scanned the area as we walked for an escape. I wanted her close in case I found an opening. She seemed to know what I was thinking and grasped her bag tighter with her other hand as she scanned the area as well.

"Shut up," Shula said and prodded me forward even though I was already moving.

If we were not in a crowded area I would have already spun around and taken out my swords. I knew I could beat Shula. However, other than cursory glances, there were no eyes on us despite me being led by knife point and Shula wearing the coat of an elite warrior, so doing that would blow our cover.

She guided us along, passed the crowds and shops, until we were near the residential ring of the village. Only then did I realize she was not taking us to the guard station or to the palace.

"Where are we going?" I asked.

She guided us to a door and urged us to open it and enter quietly. I glanced at the door, even more confused, but complied. At least inside we could get the upper hand without drawing any attention. I looked at Gesebe and when she met my eyes I raised my brows, silently telling her to get ready to run. Hopefully she understood my meaning.

The inside of the home was dark. The windows were all covered with thick curtains and the lamps with flickering flames were stationed in the corners of the rooms. It was eerily silent. I expected someone to come out of a back room and help Shula tie us up, but we were all alone. As soon as the door behind us shut, I spun around and punched Shula in the face. She stepped back in surprise and raised her hand to cover her face while her dagger hand lowered. I used the advantage and pulled out my own swords and held them at her neck. All I had to do was pull and her head would roll.

Shula felt the pressure at her neck and dropped her blade then raised her hands in surrender. To my surprise she rolled her eyes.

"Come now, let's be civil. I was not actually going to hurt you or turn you in."

I narrowed my eyes and kept my blades in the same position. Gesebe hovered behind me, ready to assist.

Shula continued. "I brought you here to ask you questions. I have been going crazy wondering what happened at the coronation. Ever since then, I have been noticing…things. I have known you for years and trained under you. You would never betray us so there must be more going on. I want you to explain. Help me understand."

I hesitated. She sounded like she was telling the truth and the look in her eyes was earnest. However, she could be lying and once we dropped our guard, she could knock us out then turn us over to my uncle.

Her being alone was odd though. She must have known I would put up a good fight and I would like to think it would take more than one warrior to bring me in.

"Be glad it was I who found you first. The guards have no idea you are here."

"Is that a threat?" I almost growled.

Her eyes widened. "Not at all. I swear Saya." This time she said Saya with conviction and respect. She clasped her hands in front of her and shook them. A sign of respect and a gesture to my authority.

What is going on? Is she telling the truth or is this some ploy?

"How did you find me?" I asked.

Shula glanced at Gesebe behind me then looked back at me. "I recognized one of the pirates from the attack on the ship weeks ago and from the coronation. Not only that but I saw Jasta with him and I knew you had to be around somewhere. And there you were, at the front leading them into the bakery rather than being towed along unlike what King Sorden would have us believe. So, I followed and waited outside Granny's."

She must be talking about Lenman. He was pretty easy to spot in a crowd what with his height, dark skin, and Drislian staff. However, anyone who had not seen him before would not think much of it. A twinge of pain entered my heart. It should not have been me leading the crew. It should have been Kip. I mentally shook off the thoughts. It was what it was, no matter how much I would like it to be otherwise.

If she had seen us before our plotting started, then she had plenty of time to call in the guards. She could have prevented this plot from ever starting. But she waited and wanted to hear my side first.

I lowered my swords but kept them out and ready. I wanted to believe Shula, and everything she had said so far sounded true, but I could never be certain. Especially after Ren unintentionally betrayed us at the mines. I could not be sure Shula was not being manipulated with skor.

"Is it alright if Gesebe searches you?" I asked.

Shula held out her arms to the side in invitation. I nodded at Gesebe, and she put her bags down before going to the warrior and searching her body for weapons and skor. After finding a couple more weapons but no skor Gesebe came to stand beside me once again. Shula gestured to the couch and chairs in the living room and we sat.

"Tell me everything," she said.

I took a leap of faith and told her everything. That was part of our mission after all. Getting more allies by telling the folks of Skorval what their Lord and King was truly up to. I told her about my kidnapping and seeing the underwater city of Under, but I left out where it was located and how the pirates got there. I recapped my adventures with the pirates through

Tripscari, Drisl, and Farlo and our attempt to free the royals from skor. That led me to explaining the true effects of skor and Lord Sorden's purpose for becoming King and how he went about doing it. Shula gasped many times throughout that part. And lastly, I explained who Kip was. I told her about his identity as true Prince of Shayd, his bravery, brilliance, and kindness, and then how he died.

Gesebe placed a hand on my arm, noticing the catch in my voice at the end of the story. We shared a sad, pained smile then turned to Shula to hear what she had to say about it all.

She sat in silence for a moment, shocked at the revelations. Then she slowly shook her head. "I had no idea."

"Not many people do, and that is why we are here. We need to stop him before he makes skor available to everyone whether it is selling it to them or putting it in their water. We need to find his lab and destroy it then we need to usurp him."

Shula nodded. "I think I can help with that. Like I said, I have been noticing some strange things and have been investigating. Not in a million years would I have suspected all that though."

"What have you discovered?" I leaned forward, eager for anything that might help us.

"First of all, there have been extra shipments going out to the other kingdoms. Skor and barrels on board with some kind of liquid inside. Not only that but I have seen invoices for receiving shipments from the other kingdoms for much less than we usually pay for them. Secondly, the royals in the castle have been acting strange."

"Strange how?" I asked.

Shula's brows furrowed. "They seem to argue quite a bit with Lord Sorden but as soon as he says something, they obey without comments. I have seen them dazedly staring at walls and frowning at their surroundings as if they are unsure where they are." She shook her head and expelled a bit of air through her nose. "At first, I thought they may be tired from their journey, but then I thought it was more than that. Now I know for sure."

I sat back and placed my elbow on the arm of the seat and rested my head in my palm as I thought about everything she just said.

"It sounds like he is using the royals to get their goods at unfair prices or even free while he ships drugged liquid to all parts of the kingdom. Soon he will control everything," I said.

"There has to be a reason he is keeping the royals here instead of letting them go back to their lands to help distribute the skor," Gesebe chimed in.

My blood ran cold and my body stiffened. "Oh my, I think I know what he is going to do, or at least a hunch."

Shula and Gesebe stared at me, waiting for me to elaborate.

"Lord Sorden was behind Kip's family's deaths and all subsequent deaths of anyone trying to rule Shayd. He is King now but that is not enough for him. He wants to be an emperor otherwise why send all that skor and liquid to the kingdoms."

Gesebe gasped, catching on to my meaning. "He is going to kill the royals," she breathed.

Shula frowned. "Well, that is a stretch, isn't it? He could just control them. Their deaths would bring about too much suspicion. And wouldn't that mean the heirs would ascend?"

I shook my head. "They have broken his control before thanks to us, so he knows that would not work long term. As for the heirs, if he got the Kings and Queens to declare him as heir then the current heirs wouldn't have a claim. Once the royals die, by accident of course," I said using my fingers to make air quotes around the word accident, "he would inherit all the lands."

"But the Kings and Queens would never allow that!" Shula exclaimed in horror.

Gesebe and I shared a look then I turned to Shula somberly. "That is the trouble with mind-controlling skor. They would not have a choice."

Shula stood quickly and started to pace. "It's been two days since they arrived. Why hasn't he done it yet?"

We were quiet for a moment trying to understand the mind of my power hungry, mind-controlling uncle.

"Maybe there is a process to getting these things done," Gesebe suggested.

"What do you mean?" I asked.

"Well…" She looked between us and trailed off. I nodded my head, silently telling her to go on. "I have run Under for years, sometimes alone since most of the Council goes to the surface often, and in that time I have noticed how much time and paperwork it takes to get anything done. And that is only for a hidden underwater city cut off from the lands above. So, I can only imagine what kind of paperwork and people would be needed to get a change like this done for all the Kingdoms. I would say we have about a week until he gets everything in order then another week before the message of his new status as heir-to-all becomes known across the Kingdoms."

"Two weeks until the Kings and Queens die," I said softly, the enormity of it all beginning to overwhelm me.

"That is, if we are guessing correctly. There is every chance the time frames we came up with are off or that might not even be his plan," Shula mentioned, coming to a stop behind the chair she had been sitting in.

I nodded. It was possible. We needed to know for sure. "We need to get a message to Oskai, Princess Edrah, and Prince Edsen inside the palace."

Shula straightened her shoulders and gripped the front of her red coat. "Consider it done."

Chapter 6

-Kip-

I reached the fork in the road an hour after the bridge. It would have been faster with a horse but obviously I did not have one and had to walk while my ribs continued to ache and my head began to pound despite the water I had been drinking to combat dehydration symptoms. I knew if I continued straight ahead, the road would lead to the Skorval mountains. My whole being wanted to take that path, but I knew there were some supplies I needed, and rest, before I could continue. I took the path that curved to the right instead and entered the village down the way.

The village was a little better than most I had seen in Shayd since arriving. None of the buildings were falling apart or boarded up. There were fresh greenery and floral arrangements lining the walkways and shops. The homes looked newer and bigger than many in the capital. Was it all because of its proximity to Skorval? The new Shayd crest flew on banners hung on every corner.

I had a feeling that if these people knew who I was, I would be in trouble. I was an excellent fighter but even I could not take on a whole town, especially while still recovering from a fall off a bridge into a ravine.

I walked around until I spotted an apothecary. I tapped the side of my coat where some coins lay and entered the shop. One other customer was inside but he was finishing his business with the shopkeeper and soon left, leaving me alone with an older man with a thick white mustache and a balding head. The man wore striped pants and vest over a long-sleeved white shirt. He looked more like a businessman than a shop owner and master of medicines.

The man looked me over and a small frown pulled his brows together but whatever he thought he kept to himself. Instead, he erased the frown by giving me a welcoming smile and leaned on the counter. "Anything I can help you with?"

Involuntarily, I covered my right side and pressed until I felt the soreness. "Some pain medication and healing elixirs if you have any."

I walked to the counter and waited as he turned to the shelves behind him. He grabbed a bottle and placed it on the counter then turned back to look for another. He rifled through a few bottles and pulled out a couple before putting them back and looking elsewhere.

"What exactly is the problem?" He asked as he continued his search.

"I…had an accident. Hurt my ribs and head pretty bad. Still recovering but I have to make it to Skorval for…uh, work." I saw an opportunity to learn about what happened to the miners and said, "I got to the Shayd mines but it looked to be abandoned so I was going to try to see if there was anything at the Skor mines." I watched him closely for a reaction.

He sighed and nodded without turning around. "I heard some of those folks saying an explosion went off in one of the mines. They cleared the place out for some time and will send in inspectors soon to see if it is safe. Some went ahead to Skorval as you are doing and some stayed here."

So, no one knew it was only a couple tiny smoke cherries. The miners were already evacuated before Sorden arrived, so it was no surprise this man had not mentioned him as part of the reason for their absence.

The man held up a bottle and studied its label. "Ah, here it is. This should help heal your ribs. Just mix a teaspoon of this in your water every 12 hours. As for your head, you do not look like you have a concussion so some pain medicine should be all you need there." He pushed both bottles to me and started to write the transaction in his shop's book.

I pulled out some coins and laid them on the counter before mixing a small amount of the healing mixture into my canteen and popping a pain pill in my mouth. Once that was done, I stuffed the bottles in an inside pocket of my coat.

"Is there a good place to eat here?" I asked.

The man took the coins and stashed them away before pointing to the right. "Follow this road down here and you will come across the tavern. Open all day, every day."

I nodded my thanks and tipped my hat at him before making my way out and in the direction he advised. He did not say the name of the tavern I should be looking for, but I realized why when I came across a large building with seats outside and open-air windows which showed the interior of the building and let the chattering and music filter into the street. There was also a sign above the door that read Tavern. So, in a way, the apothecary did tell me the name.

I nodded at the folks outside who raised their drinks toward me as a hello then I walked in. I paused in the doorway waiting for my eyes to adjust to the dim room before I could move further. The first thing I noticed was a board posted next to the door inside that had flyers and posters tacked to it. One in particular caught my attention. A wanted poster for 'The Captain' with an image of a man in a tri-pointed hat and long coat on with a sword strapped to his side. I cleared my throat and took my hat off, hoping no one would immediately recognize me without it. The face in the poster was not exact, the nose a little big and a tuft of hair on the chin that did not match reality.

Then a thought struck me. Did the apothecary know who I was? Were guards about to descend on me? I look around the room to see if anyone was pointing or alerting the owner of a rebel in their presence. I spotted people all over the room just like they were outside. Only the ones near me glanced up but they immediately went back to their conversations and meals. I did not spot anyone familiar but was not surprised by it. I barely met any miners a few days ago and did not usually get this close to Skorval when I visited Shayd. When I was confident my identity was not immediately known I found a table and settled into a seat carefully, my ribs protesting the movement.

A woman immediately stopped by with a warm smile and asked what I would like to have. I waved my hand in the air and told her anything was fine and she walked away to get it. I took the time to watch the others around me. Mostly men but a few women sat in groups around the room. They seemed happy and did not care how loud their voices got as they laughed and joked around. I wondered how many were under skor influence. I would bet all.

I overheard a conversation from a circular table about five feet away that piqued my interest. Four men and two women sat around it. Some with bowls or plates in front of them and a couple with only mugs.

"King Sorden is hiring folks to take his skor to other kingdoms and help find more business. Apparently, there are already three extra ships ready to go."

Sorden did not waste time. Unless he already had it prepared before he was crowned. He wanted to spread his stones to anyone, not just royals anymore and he planned to do it before the royals got back to their homes. That way the people would be primed to accept whatever his next plan was. I hoped the others were figuring out what that plan was and putting a stop to it. I needed to get to them soon.

A woman with chin length brown hair and brown eyes nodded next to the speaker. "I heard they get paid more than the miners who dig the stones out."

A man on the other side of her scowled. "Now how does that make sense. The miners do all the hard work while the merchants he sends out only have to ride along with the ship then speak a couple words to a few people and come back."

I knew merchants' jobs were much more than that and by the looks of his comrades they did too, but no one said anything to contradict him. I could not tell if they were supporters or disgruntled citizens fed up with Sorden.

A burly man at the table lifted his drink and took a swig before grunting and saying, "What I want to know is why are the Kings and Queens still here? Is there something we should be concerned about? A war or are they introducing the King to some secret Kingly things. It has been pretty hush hush up there."

The other woman at the table, her black hair braided and hanging in front of her reminding me a little of Ana, snorted. "You and your conspiracy theories. They are probably discussing the rebels and plans to stop them. You did hear what happened at the coronation right?"

"Yeah, but why were the young royals fighting with them?" The youngest of the group asked, quieter than the others had been this whole time.

The woman with the short brown hair leaned forward but did not try to hide her volume so others could still hear, whether on purpose or not. "King Sorden says the young have been misguided, even brainwashed by the pirates who are leading the rebels, just like they did to his heir."

The others nodded but the youngest one pursed his lips. He did not say anything though and sat back without arguing. Out of the group he seemed to be the only one who did not believe everything King Sorden was telling the public.

I listened a little longer, but their conversation veered towards personal topics and I lost interest. The woman who took my order came by a few minutes later to drop my food and drink off though I had no intention of drinking anything there in case it was laced with skor infused water or the like. Instead I placed my canteen on the table and used the water inside to quench my thirst.

I thanked her and ate my food in silence, keeping my ear out for any more information that I could glean from the townspeople without approaching them.

I was finishing up the last couple bites of my meal when two large fellows made a noisy entrance causing everyone's attention to shift to them and all conversation to cease. They were dressed in black from head to toe. One had a long coat on and the other a vest in the same color as the rest of the ensemble. The one in the long coat had dark skin and dark hair while the other was lighter and had the eyes and stature of someone native to Shayd. They looked around the room with smirks and sauntered in further until the door closed behind them. I sensed a shift in the mood of the room. People tensed and many seemed ready to flee.

"You need to leave, before I call the guards," the barkeep said from his place behind the counter.

"Is that any way to treat a customer?" The taller one with the long coat said, amused, but it was quickly followed by a sneer.

The barkeep came out from behind the counter and motioned his fellow workers back while he came to face the newcomers. "I will call the guards."

The two men snickered to each other before the one in the vest pulled out a sword and aimed it at the barkeep. "Go ahead."

I pushed my plate away and stood, reaching for my own sword and grabbing my hat with my other hand. "Men, can we not just have a peaceful meal and friendly conversation? Must we fight?"

Everyone's wide eyes shifted to me.

The barkeep shook his head and held out a hand to stop me. "Don't do it. These men are with the rebels. They have been robbing and fighting citizens in this town for a week now. They will kill you."

My eyes widened and my sword dropped a bit. They are with the rebels? That did not seem right. If they were with my crew and the people we picked up along the way then they should be in Skorval. Also, the rebels are not meant to be fighting the people. That just causes fear and mistrust and—oh, I get it.

I narrowed my eyes at the men and raised my sword back to point directly at them as I took steps forward to stand slightly in front of the barkeep. "I am sorry, sir, but you are wrong. These are mercenaries."

The barkeep's hands dropped to his sides, and he stammered, "Ho-how do you kn-know that?"

Someone from my right a few tables behind me shouted, "Mercenaries they may be, but hired by the rebels then!"

Murmurs of agreement and curses toward the rebels sounded around the room.

"No!" I kept my sword pointed at the men. "The rebels are fighting for the people. Why would they attack them and rob them instead of fighting the true enemy?"

Some people hissed the word treason at me, but I ignored them. The barkeep frowned and crossed his arms as if that would block the words I was saying.

I focused my attention back on the mercenaries. "You two need to leave and do not come back to this town. Leave the citizens of Shayd alone."

The taller, darker skinned man sneered. "Or what?"

"You will have me to deal with."

The shorter man laughed and beat the side of my blade with his sword, trying to knock it away. My training took over and I repositioned my sword by ducking it under the man's blade and stepped forward until the tip rested against the shorter man's throat. I kept my arm extended and my body set so my right foot was aimed toward him, but the front of my body faced the wall to my left effectively limiting the target area they could attack.

"Who are you?" he asked, glaring at me as he lowered his sword.

"You mean you do not recognize me?"

The two men shared confused glances. I smirked and put my hat on then reached over to rip the wanted poster off the wall next to them since they were still standing near the door and held it up next to my face.

"I am the Captain. Otherwise known as Prince Kipsien of Shayd."

Behind me, gasps and murmurs filled the room, some excited and shocked while others were disbelieving and angry. The two men in front of me frowned and tensed which made me tense, ready for a fight. I had to get them outside, so we did not destroy the tavern or injure any civilians.

In one swift move, the taller mercenary pulled a dagger from behind his long, black, coat and swiped at me. I leaned back which gave the shorter man enough time to get away from my blade and raise his own in defense. Gasps and frightened shouts sounded behind me.

I beat the sword away from me and kicked the vested mercenary in the chest, making him stumble out of the tavern leaving me to face the other one with the dagger. I stabbed at him, but he parried with his dagger. We continued that dance for a minute, but he parried every attack. However, each time I took I step forward he stepped back until we were both outside, so I at least got something out of the fight.

As soon as I stepped outside, the other man who had apparently been waiting for me attacked from the side, and I had to leap to my left to avoid the strike. The two mercenaries attacked at the same time, but I was skilled in swordplay, so I easily parried their moves. I calculated I could take both down in five moves and slid my foot forward and twisted it to the side as my first step to accomplishing it.

The door behind me slammed open and the customers from the tavern poured out to form a half circle around us. They watched with wide, frightened and curious eyes as I faced the two mercenaries.

Briefly I heard someone in the crowd say, "If they are rebels or hired by the rebels then why is the leader of the rebels fighting them?"

I smiled. Finally, someone was asking the right questions.

Dagger man lunged forward and thrusted his blade out, but I had already anticipated the move and my foot was in the position to make spinning easier. As I spun around him, I used the pommel of my blade to hit his back making him stumble forward. That was step two.

While he was regaining his balance, I faced the vested man but kept the other one in my line of sight so as not to be snuck upon. The man attacked with fierce strikes all of which I was able to avoid. When I saw an opening, I sliced at his wrist making him drop his sword. The man hissed at the pain and cradled his wrist.

With step three complete I turned to the other man just in time to block another stab. Using the same move I did on his friend, I sliced at his wrist when an opening presented itself making him drop his blade. Unlike the other one, this man did not stop to hold his wrist. He yelled and ran at me, attempting to tackle me. I braced myself then moved to the side at the last second and stuck my foot out making him trip on his way passed me. That was not the step five I had in my mind, but it worked out all the same.

I turned now that both men were on the same side and pointed my weapon at them. The man I tripped seemed to have gotten his footing which I was a little disappointed about. I would have liked to see him sprawled out on the ground.

"Barkeep," I called over my shoulder. When I heard the crunch of his boots behind me, I continued. "Where do you lock up criminals in this town?"

There was a pause as the man decided whether to tell me, a rebel leader, but seemed to think he hated the men in front of me more than me at the moment. "Xekiel keeps 'em until transport can get here to take 'em to Skorval."

"Have a few people take these men to him then."

I did not see what the barkeep did behind me, but it must have been some kind of signal because four men from the crowd came over and each one gripped one of the arms of the mercenaries then hauled them away to wherever this Xekiel person was.

I finally lowered my sword and went to turn to the crowd, but I did not get all the way around before something heavy smashed into the side of my head. I went down hard and my vision started to go black. I groaned and tried to touch the spot where I had been hit to assess the damage, but my arms were suddenly held tight by a couple of men and I was hauled to a standing position. My head lolled and my body threatened to give out.

The barkeep came close though he was a bit fuzzy to me, everything was. "They may not work for you and you may have saved us from them but you are still a wanted man and the King will pay handsomely for your capture."

I growled but it turned out as more of a groan. The men led me away without another word.

75

Chapter 7

-Ana-

With Shula gone to find the Drislian siblings and pass on our hunches, Gesebe and I used Shula's place as a base of operations. We were in charge of the inner ring of the town which meant we had to talk to those in the market, main square, and visitors from other places since most came to the center of the town to do business or visit. It would be difficult because the main square had more guards than the other rings. I drew out a rough map on a piece of parchment and together, Gesebe and I laid out a plan.

It was not until the next day that we were able to begin.

I knew only talking to the citizens of Skorval and Shayd would be the equivalent of spreading rumors and there was no reason for anyone to follow us based on word of mouth and status alone. However, if it put even a little doubt in their minds about Sorden than I would count it as success. If I used logic, then I was sure I could make enough people second guess their King and start to notice what he was doing right under their noses.

First stop was the local watering station. There was a large cistern near one of the mountains that fed water into the town through a series of underground pipes. The pipes were made when Shayd metal was our biggest commodity. Shayd metal was the best in all the lands because it was tougher than any other kind and flexible. It could withstand any type of temperature or weather and was smooth. The Shayd mines still produced ore for the metal but since Sorden had become leader the trade had shifted to skor.

However, because the cistern and pipes were made of Shayd metal, it would be difficult to destroy them, so we had to do the next best thing and destroy the water stations which were just pulleys that brought the water up into a spout from the pipes.

Gesebe and I were dressed like the other citizens in town, so we got to the stations without notice. I counted three guards in the area. We could take them if need be but our best chances were to not be seen. People were rushing about in all directions, so it was easy to hide among them. Everyone wanted or needed water and they carried buckets with them to take back to their homes or shops. In the inner ring, it was most likely needed for their places of business. Each ring had a station so there was not much need for them to come to this station if it was for their homes. Five spouts were lined up along a wall and there were lines for each one. We would need to hit all of them.

It sounded as if we were cutting off their supply of water which could make people die from dehydration or cause issues in businesses that relied on water. However, there was a freshwater river, albeit a small one, that ran along the outer rings and a small lake that collected water from runoffs near the edge of each mountain in Skorval. It would be stressful and difficult for the inner rings, but they could still get water and that way, they would not be drinking from skor-laced cistern water.

I gave a single nod to Gesebe who nodded back from across the station. We each had one flash rock and a couple blast cherries that Gesebe brought along from their stash in Under. Lenman created the devices. He called one of them a cherry due to their round, red shape and thin stem that acted as a fuse. He also created smoke cherries which we had used in the Shayd mines to evacuate everyone.

At the same time, we threw the flash rocks at an open area. It would not harm anyone, but it was loud and it was bright. As the light and sound exploded across the station people started to scream and run in every direction. We used the pandemonium to push closer to the water pumps and lay out our blast cherries. Kip had done the same thing to the well at the Shayd mines, making the miners get their water from the running water nearby which was nearly impossible to drug with skor.

As soon as we laid them out and ripped the stems off, we rushed to a safe distance and watched the destruction.

One. Two. Three. Four.

Stone flew through the air and the ground was practically a hole around where each one exploded. It would not be able to get fixed for a few days which would be enough time for the skor to leave the people's systems.

"Ana, we missed one," Gesebe said loud enough for me to hear her over the screaming. She pointed at the middle pump. She had only given me two cherries to use so I assumed she would have the other three.

As if reading my mind, she leaned in and said, "I only had four blast cherries, the others are smoke ones."

The guards had their swords out and were going over to investigate. We did not have time to worry about the last one. It would make things a little difficult because people could still access water from there, but we had to take what we could get.

I pulled her arm so she would follow me and we joined the crowd leaving the station and made our way to the main square.

Part one was done, now we just had to spread the story and sow doubt. When the time came to confront Sorden, if it led to battle, then we hoped to have enough loyal followers to win. We started with Merchants Row. This was the area in the main square where the stalls were temporary, and each morning they were set up for the day or taken down so the owner could move on to the next town. By starting there, we could spread the story further.

It was already crowded with people: merchants, customers, and guards. Stalls lined both sides of the road and merchants waved their wares at passersby to get their attention. I took a moment to take it all in. It was not often that I came down from the palace to check out the wares of the merchants but when I did, I always felt invigorated with their energy and enthusiasm.

I smiled at Gesebe and dipped my head toward the right side, giving her a silent order to go that way then I hooked my thumb at the left and pointed to myself indicating I would go that way. She nodded and split from me. She was so short that she immediately got swallowed by the crowd and I lost sight of her. I knew she was capable of handling herself and did not worry, but I still hesitated a moment before going my own way.

I met the eyes of the man at the first stall on the left which on Merchant's Row, meeting the merchants' eyes was usually a bad idea. The first sign of attention you give them, and they descend like a pack of hounds. This time however, I held his stare which encouraged him to approach me and start trying to promote his products. He was a rug weaver and I had to admit they were beautiful rugs, but that was not why I was there.

"Please, please, come over," he gestured then started rambling. "These are made of all kinds of materials. Are you interested in wool? Cotton? I even have Drislian silk rugs." That seemed impractical but eh, what do I know about rugs? "I brought some all the way from the Tripscari Islands and a few of these brighter colored and more airy ones are from Farlo. All made by me and my team across the kingdoms." He grinned and spread his hands to indicate all the rugs in his stall.

I perused the various kinds of rugs as he watched me like an eager hawk. I ran my fingers over a few of them, feeling the texture. Though impractical as a rug, the Drislian silk cloths could be used as a tapestry to hang on the walls. They were beautiful and smooth with a main image of an animal or flower in the middle and patterns along the edges. Being made of Drislian silk meant it would be expensive though.

Looking at the various patterns gave me an idea and I turned back to the merchant who stood a little taller and continued grinning. I briefly wondered if his jaw hurt at the end of each encounter with a customer.

"Do you do commissions?" I asked.

The merchant nodded and pointed to a purple and white rug with tassels at each end. "This one is a commission done for a shop owner. He will be picking it up today. What are you looking for?" He grabbed a piece of paper from a satchel and a quill and readied his hand to take my order specifications.

I did not plan on actually ordering a rug but this lead me into the start of what I needed to tell him and others.

"Can you put an image of the Shayd crest in the middle of it?"

The man nodded and began scribbling on his sheet.

"The original one? The compass crest?" I watched him for a reaction, and he did not disappoint.

His hand stilled and he quickly looked around to make sure what I said was not heard by anyone, but the area was so busy no one was paying us any attention. The man straightened and held his quill loosely by his side.

I stared at him innocently and continued. "You know, the crest never should have changed. The compass crest has a long history and the true heir, Prince Kipsien, did not appreciate his family being forgotten like that. I mean, what does this new one represent? Complete control and no free will? That is what skor does to people. It breaks your mind," I emphasized that last line by tapping my head.

He crossed his arms and narrowed his eyes. "I think our business is done here." He said it but his glance around made me wonder if he believed me and just did not want trouble or if he was truly loyal to Sorden.

He did not look like he was from Shayd, well maybe a little bit around the eyes and height, but his skin tone was that of the Islands—mixed, like me.

"Where are you from?" I asked, ignoring his comment.

He narrowed his eyes but answered, finding no harm in telling me. "Tripscari. But I travel all over for business."

I nodded and smiled knowingly. "Then you must know that King Trost was not a fan of Lord Sorden and banned skor from his islands." The man nodded slowly, wondering where I was going with my statement. "He knew that there was something wrong with the skor. Have you heard about what happened at the coronation?" Another slow nod. "Well, then you know the Princes and Princess fought against their parents. Why would they do that unless something was wrong? Let me tell you this then I will leave. Do not touch skor and do not drink anything from public water places." I bowed my head and turn to leave. "Thank you for listening."

The thoughtful frown he showed before I left gave me hope he would think about it. That merchant would probably be the easiest to talk to today. Being from Tripscari meant he was probably already wary of skor due to it being banned from Tripscari but now he could start thinking about everything else such as the events from the coronation, the rebellion, the skor trade picking up, and the way people were behaving.

I continued the same story down the line of merchants, stopping at each stall whether it was busy or not and finding some way to introduce the truth to those nearby. Their reactions varied but the majority were upset and threatened to call the guards if I continued spreading my treasonous lies.

They did not outright call them over because it would cause drama near their stall and make them lose business, so I used that to my advantage and completed what I had to say before moving on. More than a few customers gave me curious glances and I heard some whispers wondering who I was. Without my red coat identifying me as an elite Skorval warrior and my hair freed of its classic braid, they did not recognize me. That just proved once again that I should have visited the town more.

After the last stall I looked around for Gesebe and spotted her waiting near an alleyway standing on a crate so we would be able to see each other. I walked over, glancing around to make sure the guards had not been alerted.

She saw me coming and stepped down from her perch. "How did it go?" she asked.

"As expected. We only got started and I already feel like we are wasting our time."

She hummed in agreement.

"Yours did not go so well either?"

She shook her head and let out a weary sigh. "Without the Captain or skor, we have no way to prove our story. It is just hearsay."

"A little doubt can go a long way." I patted her on the shoulder then steered her away from Merchant's Row. "Let us go get something to eat and start again in the other parts of this circle."

We got to Granny's in no time, the café/bakery being close by and in the heart of the Skorval town which was where we would start next.

I sat down with some cocoa and a couple sandwiches and Gesebe cradled a cup of juice made from a tropical fruit found in Tripscari and had a bagel in front of her. There were a few people in the shop, some perusing the baked goods and others sat at the tables on the right eating their food and talking quietly. No one paid us any attention, but I had a feeling after today we would get stares wherever we went if not arrested.

"I have decided," I whispered. Gesebe leaned forward and waited for me to continue. "After we are done here today, I am going to go to the mines and help Jasta find proof of the lab."

Gesebe's eyes widened, and she shook her head. "You're going to leave me alone?" She looked dismayed, as if being left out of another mission.

I placed my hand on her arm and squeezed reassuringly. "I will have Shula help you. Having an elite guard would help give you credibility too."

She frowned and looked down at her cup of juice. "I don't like it…but I trust you. I will stay down here, but as soon as I am done in this circle, I am coming for you."

I shook my head. "No, you need to check on the others. When they are done with their rings, they should be coming into the center ring to check in. You can send Shula to me for updates after that if need be."

"Whatever you say," Gesebe grumbled uncharacteristically. She nibbled on her bagel quietly for the rest of our break and avoided looking at me directly.

I sighed and wished I could make her happier, but I could not change her directive. She still had a mission down here, but I needed to check on things up the mountain and see if we could move things along.

Chapter 8

-Kip-

It took a while for my senses to clear enough that I could take in my surroundings. A lump on my head throbbed and I touched it, wincing as my fingers encountered the sore spot. I was propped up against a cot and a wall surrounded by wooden boards. It seemed it was a makeshift holding cell. Usually, the bigger towns had metal cells. I could probably break through this one, but I did not have enough energy right now or blast cherries. I stood up, using the cot as support and stumbled to the wooden boards being used as bars.

Each board was wide, leaving only little slits in between each one. I peered through one of the slits at the front of the cell and saw a small room lit by a candle though sunlight still streamed in through the gaps in closed shutters on the left. Underneath the window was an unkempt bed. A desk sat perpendicular to the wall across from me but too far to reach and on top was my sword. They left me with the rest of my belongings, including my signet ring, which I was relieved to find. I walked to my right and peered through the boards at that side of the room. There was about a three-foot gap then another cell. I did not hear anything, making me wonder if it was empty or if the mercenaries were in that one unconscious.

Since no one was moving about I decided to try to escape quietly. I tried the door, and it rattled slightly, the sound of metal on wood. I could not see what kind of lock it was and had nothing to pick it even if I did see it, so I looked around some more, trying to find a weak point. I pressed on the top, middle, and bottom of each board but there was no give in any. That left only force which would make a lot of noise. I peered through a slit again but still did not see anyone. Alright then, best give it a try. I aimed my shoulder at a board to the left of the door, took a few steps back then ran straight at the wood. My shoulder hit it, sending pain reverberating across my arm and back. I hissed and rubbed at my shoulder until the pain started to go away while I watched the wood. The sound had been loud, but I heard no cracks. Looking closer, I did not see any either. I tried a few more times on the same piece, hoping to weaken it. I switched shoulders after two more times and did it again.

"Oi!"

I froze at the sound of the voice. It came from in front of me somewhere, not to the right where the other cell was, so it must be someone else.

"Cut it out. I don't need to be hearing all that racket."

I peered through one of the slits and saw a man with curly, long, messy black hair, in simple commoner garb. He had his hands on his hips and glared at me. His glare was made harsher by the scar running through his right eye and stretching above his eyebrow.

"Are you Xekiel?" I asked.

He curled his lip. "What of it?"

"Are the mercenaries in the other cell?" I asked, ignoring his ire.

He glanced to his left—my right—then back at me and nodded. Then he sneered, upset that he was friendly enough to answer my question. "You lot will soon be in Skorval so don't get too comfortable and don't hurt yourself trying to escape, I made these myself." He looked proud and I wondered what his profession was when he wasn't looking after belligerents in here but doubted he would answer me if I asked so I sulked back to my cot and sat down, trying to figure out what to do next.

A knock sounded at the door. Xekiel had disappeared to wherever he had been before he berated me yet still within hearing distance. He came out from that place and answered the door. The boards on my cell were too thick so I could not see who it was, but I could hear their conversation.

"I have come for the prisoner known as the Captain."

There was a pause then Xekiel's doubtful voice answered, "Barent, I know you are not a guard and I know your mother will be angry to know you came here looking for a peek at our infamous rebel."

"I-I was tasked to bring the Captain to—" The man at the door tried again. He sounded young and familiar but without seeing him I could not place where I had heard him before.

Xekiel laughed. "Go on now, Barent. If you were here to take him under orders you would have papers and backup. There is no way a scrawny boy like you could take him alone. You'd be dead in a ditch in a minute."

I heard the creak of the door then a slap on the wood of it. I tried to see what was happening but could not from this angle. It sounded like Xekiel tried to close the door and something stopped it.

"I am not a boy," the person at the door said angrily.

Xekiel sighed. "Barent, I am sorry, but you need to go. I will have to tell your mother about this."

A heavy thump and cursing. Through the slit in the wood of my cell I watched as two people, Xekiel and another younger man, fell to the floor.

The man that was presumably Barent stood quickly and apologized. "I'm sorry, I tripped, I didn't mean to knock you over."

Xekiel stood and grabbed Barent by the shoulder and moved him back to the door and out of my sight.

The door slammed shut a second later and Xekiel grumbled under his breath, his voice getting farther away as he moved back to the other room he had been in before the arrival.

Hours passed. At some point, Xekiel brought me a piece of bread, some soup, and a tin can of water. Again, I avoided the water in case it was laced with skor, although my canteen was practically empty by now. I heard him go to the other cell to give the others the same. The mercenaries had awoken an hour before the food came and had been talking quietly among themselves. I did not call out or talk to myself so the others might not have known I was there.

The light from the window was lessening and shadows crept into the room to start filling every space. I laid on my cot for a while but dared not sleep. I needed a way out and I figured the best time would be at night, however, that bed I saw earlier meant Xekiel would stay here and getting out would be difficult. Maybe my best bet would be to overpower the guards when they came to take me away or somehow escape on the journey to Skorval which meant I would have to stay here until that happened.

More time passed and the night creatures made their presence known by howling or hooting outside. Only a small candle flickered on the table, so my cell was mostly dark. I heard snoring in the other cell. They had either fallen asleep or were faking it as they attempted to find a way to escape. I did not know either way. Xekiel finally came in and started shuffling around, preparing for bed. I heard him groan contentedly as he settled into his bed, but he left the candle lit.

A loud noise outside the window shattered the night. It was like glass breaking. Xekiel cursed and got up from his bed. I heard him go to the window and curse again.

"Fire. Who in the world—?"

Another bit of glass broke and suddenly I saw orange light fill the room, brighter than the candlelight and from near the window. Was the room on fire?

Xekiel continued to curse as he put his boots on and grabbed a bucket and headed for the door.

"Wait, you are just going to leave us here?" I shouted after him.

The snoring in the other cell ceased and I heard confused grumbling from the two men in it. Once they realized what was happening, they started beating at the boards and shouting for Xekiel to release them.

"Quiet, the lot of you! The fire is outside, not yet reached the building. I will deal with it."

With that, Xekiel left us alone and we were quiet as we listened for the sounds outside.

Then the others grew impatient.

"Forget waiting! Now is our chance!"

I heard them grunt and growl as they slammed into the wooden boards of their cell. It made quite the racket, but the fire outside was loud enough to disguise it from Xekiel. I tested the wood of each board, knowing ramming against it did not work last time. I did not bother telling the mercenaries that. They would ignore me and do it anyway.

I reached my hand as far as it would go through the slit at the door to my cell and felt for the lock. The slit was small so only four of my fingers would fit, stopping my hand once it reached the top of my palm. My fingers brushed the lock, it seemed like it was a simple padlock, easy to pick if only I had the maneuverability to do it.

"Let me do that for you."

I yanked my hand back, startled at the voice on the other side of the door and leaned forward slowly to see who it was. The man from earlier, Barent, beamed at me as he held up a key and moved forward to unlock the lock.

A second later, I heard the padlock click and removed from the wood then door swung open. I stepped out cautiously, and glanced to my left and right, all the while keeping the stranger within my line of sight.

The fire to my left could be seen out the window though it was far enough from the house that it was no worry yet. I could not see Xekiel but assumed he was out there throwing buckets of water onto it.

To my right, the mercenaries continued pounding on the boards in their cell, unaware that a man just freed me with the key.

"Who are you?" I asked with narrowed eyes. I walked forward, twisting to keep him in sight, and grabbed my sword from the table.

"I will explain everything, but first we should get out of here before Xekiel comes back."

He headed for the exit, not waiting to see if I would follow and left through the open doorway. I hesitated for only a moment then jogged to catch up to him. The men in the other cell still had not heard us over the fire and their own commotion.

The night was dark, and this location was far enough from town that the lights from the street lamps did not reach here to light our way. It did not matter though because my companion seemed to know where he was going.

We walked for a while, not daring to slow down yet. I stopped hearing the noises from Xekiel's place but that did not mean he would not come after us which meant we still needed to get farther away. The distant lights grew dimmer with each step, and I realized we were heading away from town even more. I knew we had to be quiet as we escaped so I held in my burning questions for when we eventually stopped.

Finally, a while later, the stranger gripped my arm and pulled me to the side and into a thicket of tress.

His breath brushed my ear as he whispered near it, "We should be safe here for tonight."

I heard rustling and could barely make out his movements under the moonlight that shone through the thick canopy. I found a relatively flat area and sat down, my back resting against a tree trunk.

"Who are you?" I whispered. Whispers in the night seemed to be how our conversation was going to happen, but it was that or continue holding in my questions. "Why did you break me out?"

"You're welcome, first of all—"

"Right," I may not have known who this was, but he had rescued me, "Thank you."

"And secondly, I saw you in the tavern and heard about what you have been doing here in Shayd. My cousin was at the coronation. He told me all about the fight. I am not quite sure what you have against King—I mean, Lord Sorden, but whatever it is it looks like you need to be free to continue fighting."

I was quiet as I turned over his words in my mind. He had seen me in the tavern. Realization dawned and I shook my finger at him even though he could not see. He was the young man at the table who was questioning everything his friends said. Although, even if he questioned Lord Sorden in the tavern and questioned the fight at the coronation, why did he think we were the right choice? Why did he think I was?

"My name is Barent. Do I call you the Captain then? Or Your Highness?"

"Kip will do."

"Kip," he said to himself, trying out the name. "Nice to meet you, Kip."

"Likewise." I hesitated for a moment but decided it was better to ask rather than assume. "What are your plans now that I am free?"

He chuckled. "I could ask you the same thing."

I stayed quiet, not giving anything away until he did.

He sighed. "I am not sure yet. I started the fire and freed a prisoner so I should be considered an outlaw, but no one saw me so I could probably go back, and no one would be the wiser."

"I hear a but…" I said prompting him to continue.

"But," he said drawing out the word, "I feel stifled in that town. Everyone sees me as a boy still despite having turned eighteen two months ago. I want to help you on your journey. The Princes and Princess as well as our own Saya, the heir of Sorden, fought against the new King at the coronation. There must be a good reason and I want to help."

"What have you heard about why we fight?"

"Well…" He hesitated, "My cousin said you declared yourself the Prince of Shayd and are backed by powerful people who claim it is true. I figure you are wanting your throne back."

"And you would help us just for that reason? You do not know me."

"Like I said, the others who fight alongside you are powerful people, and they must have a good reason."

"What about the Kings and Queens who support Lord Sorden? They are powerful people too," I pointed out.

He was silent for a few moments. If he made any movements, I did not see it due to the darkness. Finally, he said, "Tell me why you fight. Help me understand the division in our lands."

So, I told him everything. Well, almost everything. I left out the part about Under and the people protected there from all this 'division' here on land. And I did not exactly tell him about the skor. He lived in the town closest to Sorden. I could not be sure he was not influenced, despite his actions pointing to the opposite so far. I would wait a couple days for it to leave his system then tell him. So, I told him about raiding Skorval ships, meeting Ana, our mission to break the people away from Sorden's control, though I left out the part about how they were being controlled. I even told him about the mercenaries behind my family's death and who hired them.

When I finished, he whistled long and low. "So, it is not to take your throne back."

"Not in the beginning but I cannot help but feeling like that is part of why I fight now. Stopping Sorden's control and deposing him is my first goal but after that, I think it is time to take my place. I have hidden away long enough."

Barent was quiet as he mulled over my words.

I shifted until I was laying down, using my arm as a head rest then shut my eyes. "Let us get some sleep. If you decide in the morning you still want to help, then we will head for Skorval together."

"Goodnight, Your Highness."

I did not correct him on the title.

Chapter 9

-Ana-

$\mathcal{I}$ left Gesebe at Shula's house the next day and told her I would send the warrior when I found her if she did not make it back before then. I reminded her that we were to also look for skor and destroy it to which she nodded grumpily, still upset she could not go with me. We had not had any more luck in the other parts of the inner ring. The guards were called on us twice, but we escaped through the crowds and ducked into shops to avoid them. I did not know what we could do down here to make the people trust us. I needed to find Jasta and that lab and have it destroyed before those shipments went out. Otherwise, everyone would be under my uncle's will.

The mines were not on the same mountain as the palace which was on the eastern mountain near the ocean. The mines were on the northwestern mountain, the farthest away from the borders of Skorval and the sea. I did not go there much growing up, but I knew to get to it I had to use the same pulleys and platforms as visitors coming into Skorval had to use on the southwest mountain.

It took nearly half a day to reach the platforms and be lifted up to the various entrances to the mines. The guards were bored and half dazed with drink so they did not give me a second glance as I went up.

Now, where to find Jasta and the others?

The mines were a maze and had three levels to explore. I was on the first level and in front of me were four openings leading to different tunnels. I had no idea where to start so I just picked the far right one and went in, hoping to find one of them on the way.

It was dark inside but every few feet were torches set in the wall. The temperature significantly lowered the farther I ventured until I wished for my coat. There was no one nearby for quite some time but the noise of distant pounding and clanking reverberated through the tunnel.

That noise got louder, and I followed it until the tunnel opened up into a large circular area. About twenty people piled blue-green stones into carts, dug into walls with pickaxes and other tools, and moved about doing other mining tasks that I was not familiar with. I scanned their faces for a familiar one but did not see any. Another tunnel branched off in the back to another part of the mountain and I realized this was going to take forever.

I walked up to the nearest worker and tapped their shoulder. She was a middle-aged woman, her hair in disarray and dirt marks on various parts of her skin. She had on a hard hat and was working near one of the carts.

She turned to me with impatience sparking in her eyes and a hand on her hip. "What do you need?" She asked gruffly.

I looked around the room, continuing to look for my friends then turned back to her. "Where are the new recruits?"

She eyed me up and down then chuckled and shook her head. "You're late."

"What?" I frowned at her, not understanding what she thought she picked up on.

"You know, if you want to keep this job, showing up late and not knowing where to report will get you

103

kicked out real fast. Luckily for you, I am not a supervisor." She glanced to a man with a clipboard at a different cart and raised her brow at me.

Ah, she thought I was one of the new recruits just looking for my group. Well, it was a good cover, so I went with it. I rolled my eyes and smiled. "Totally. I understand. It will not happen again."

She pursed her lips, unbelieving, but pointed to the tunnel at the back of the room. "Take that tunnel then turn left. You should have taken the second tunnel coming in, but this will get you there too. You will continue down, passing that room, and go into the next tunnel until you get to the room there. That's where they should be."

I murmured her instructions, committing them to memory then nodded my thanks and headed for the place she pointed to. I could only hope she was right.

The tunnel to the left was empty but it led to a full room, busier than the one I left. I know the woman said the new recruits were another tunnel further, but I took a couple minutes to look around for familiar faces anyway. Again, none that I could readily identify though a couple looked like those from the Shayd mines. Maybe they were a part of the group called in to help the rebels or displaced workers from our fake explosion. I continued on, no one giving me a second glance when I passed them and moved on to the next room.

This room was nearly identical to the rest, but the group of people were not spread out. They were all gathered around a cart at the back of the room, meaning it was obvious when I entered. They turned to look at me when I got close, and I took that moment to quickly scan their faces. Relief flooded me when I spotted Ren and Lenman. They were both the tallest people in the room, so it was not too hard to spot them. They were both dressed in common garb with a hardhat and various tools on their belts. Knowing Lenman, he probably had gadgets hidden among his person. Their eyes widened when they saw me then glanced at each other.

An older man who was facing their small group peered around the people in front of him and scowled at me. "You. What do you want? I am busy training these recruits."

I smiled apologetically and walked faster until I was among the group. "I got lost. I am supposed to be part of the group."

"You're late. Don't let it happen again." With that scolding statement, he dismissed me and went back to instructing everyone.

I moved closer to Ren, trying not to draw the Overseer's notice, and bumped his arm. He looked down at me and arched his brow in silent questioning of my presence.

As quiet as I could, I whispered, "Where is Jasta?"

Ren did not answer for a moment, waiting until he knew he could get away with answering before leaning down and whispering, "Second level. That is all I know. She will check in at the end of the day."

I thought about going to the second floor and looking for her, but I already had difficulty finding the recruits so finding Jasta, especially if she wanted to stay hidden, would be nearly impossible. I decided to stay with them the rest of the day and wait for Jasta's report. Which meant I would be mining skor for the day. Sounded counterproductive to our goals but it gave me an idea of how to sabotage production. I just needed to find a time to talk to Lenman and Ren alone.

After a bit more instruction about how to use one of the tools, the Overseer gave us our tasks and slowly walked among us to check our progress. I was assigned to a cart since I was late and had missed most of the instruction. That was fine by me though because I was going to try to find a way to be stationed at a cart anyway and this worked out.

The day went on, mostly silent among us due to the Overseer's watch though I thought normally, miners were not this quiet. Occasionally, I caught Lenman and Ren's eyes, theirs questioning and mine trying to convey needing to meet with them.

Eventually, Lenman brought a bucket over to the cart as others had been doing for hours now. Instead of dumping the bucket of stones into the cart he took them out one at a time to give us a chance to talk.

I counted the load on a clipboard and weighed the cart as it started to fill up. Whispering I asked, "Where does this cart go?"

Lenman looked around subtly and seeing we were alone, answered, "They take it to a storage area somewhere along this line," he gestured to the tracks the cart was on, "and someone there loads them into barrels. At least that is what the Overseer claimed."

"I need to find where this goes. If I can destroy the supply, it might slow down his plans."

Lenman leaned down to grab another stone from his bucket and whispered, "What do you know of his plans? Is that why you are here instead of in the town?"

I looked around to find the Overseer to make sure he had not seen our work lacking. He was teaching someone how to hold their pickaxe correctly and currently had his back to us.

"I do not know anything for sure, but an informant told me of his extra shipments going out to the other kingdoms this week. If we can slow that down, we might have a chance to stop this before it is distributed everywhere. We also need to find the lab quickly and figure out how he is changing these," I point to the raw stones in the cart, "to mind controlling objects."

Lenman nodded and stood straighter with his now empty bucket. "I will talk to Ren, and we will come up with something. Stay with the cart and follow it to the end of the line to find the rest."

That was already my plan, but I nodded anyway, and we continued with our work until the Overseer called for a much-needed break. Everyone shuffled toward a back tunnel and murmured about food and what would be for dinner. I assumed the dining room for the miners was through that tunnel then and while I was hungry, I figured this would be a great opportunity to find the storage room.

Lenman and Ren found me, noticed I was lagging behind, and caught on quick. We waited for the Overseer and the rest of the miners to pass us then doubled back to the room and entered through a different tunnel, following the tracks for the cart.

It took a while, and we stayed silent the whole way so as not to attract unwanted attention but eventually came to a large, round, closed door. It had a lock in the middle of the door that would need a large key to open. I guessed only certain people were allowed access to the storage room. We would need the key to get in, unless we wanted to blow it up but when I got closer and placed my hand on the metal, I could tell it was a special material, Shayd metal, which meant it would be near impossible to break through.

I sighed and turned to my friends. "I guess that is it then. The Overseer must have the key. Who does he send to the storage room to deposit the cart?"

Ren shrugged but Lenman answered, "Yesterday it was one of the recruits escorted by someone from a different room."

I nodded thoughtfully. "I am going to have to make sure it is me today. I need to see inside."

Lenman studied the door and must have come to the same conclusion about the metal because he did not offer to blow it up.

"Let us head back then and eat, wait it out, until the end of the day," Ren advised.

We nodded our agreement and headed back the way we came.

We arrived in a large room that was bustling with hungry miners. Rows and rows of long tables were set in the middle and along the left were three lines of people waiting to get their food. There were definitely more than just the recruits in there. It looked like the whole first level was in there.

We stood in one of three lines and got our food which consisted of potatoes, a roll, juice, and a leg of some bird. Turkey, I would guess, due to the size. We found a few seats at the end of one of the long tables. It was near impossible to find a space that was away from everyone, but we made do with what was available.

The men were silent while they ate but I knew the questions would come so I cut to the point and explained my first day in Skorval in the towns trying to convince people and meeting up with one of my warriors. I spoke in between bites of my food but it was not a long story, so it was not long until I got to the part where I arrived at the mines.

Lenman took a drink from his glass bottle of juice and frowned at me. "You left Gesebe alone?"

Gesebe and Lenman were both Council members for Under and he knew Gesebe had never really ventured on missions with them before, so I understood his concern. But I also knew Gesebe was resourceful and determined to help. I knew she could handle herself. Plus, Shula should be making her way back down to the town soon and would be with her.

"She is fine. What we need to do is find that lab and stop those shipments. How is Jasta? Does she remember?"

It had been years since Jasta was ran out by Sorden for finding his lab and she had found it accidentally. I would be surprised and impressed if she found it the first day.

"She said something about it being on the second level but is still searching for it," Lenman answered.

"What is everyone else doing then?" I asked, remembering they came with a group of rebels.

Ren and Lenman glanced at each other then back to me.

"They are blending until our signal then they are advised to..." Ren paused and smiled to himself before continuing, "let chaos reign."

Lenman rolled his eyes at his partner's theatrics and explained, "They will cause as much destruction and upheaval as possible without getting anyone hurt. It will draw attention away from the palace and then Oskai and the others can sneak out the Kings and Queens."

I nodded. It was a good plan. I wondered when they planned it with the palace rebels and why I was not told of it before now.

Ren must have seen something of that thought on my face because he laid a hand on my arm reassuringly and said, "We would have sent someone to tell you before the chaos started."

I gave him a half smile and we went back to eating.

The Overseer called us back to work ten minutes later and for the rest of the day we worked on mining skor and filling the cart. It was tiring work and by the end I was ready to pass out. I knew some of the miners would sleep in the cabins at the bottom of the mountain and some would sleep in tents up here on the sides of the mines. Others would trek down into the outer ring of Skorval to their residences. I assumed since we had not been there long we were relegated to the tents until more permanent accommodations could be made.

However, I knew when the Overseer called it a day that I could not go to the tents because I had to convince the Overseer to let me take the cart.

People started shuffling off, done with the day and ready for sleep. Ren and Lenman hung back to meet me, but I tilted my head to the cart. Lenman signaled they would wait outside, and they left.

I went to the Overseer who did not look up when I approached. I knew he saw me though because he asked in a bored tone, "What do you want?"

"I was hoping I could take the cart to the holding room."

At that, he looked up and narrowed his eyes. "You were the one who was late today, right?" He ended it as a question, but I knew it was rhetorical. "Why should I give you that responsibility?"

Seeing my opening I raised a finger and confidently said, "That is exactly why you should give me the job. I need to prove that I can be responsible, and that tardiness was only a one-time mistake. Also, I was with the cart most of the day so I might as well finish it to the end."

He studied me for a long moment. I straightened my shoulders to give off an air of confidence and responsibility. If only he knew who he was talking to.

"Fine." Then he shouted to someone I did not realize had entered the room. "Torin, go with her to the storage room." He took a key from around his neck and handed it to Torin when the man got close. I eyed the man out of the corner of my eye and tried not to feel offended that I had a babysitter for this task. I remembered Lenman saying each recruit was paired with a more veteran worker to escort the skor to the storage room which made me relax a little.

Torin was young, maybe around my age or a little older with dirt smudged cheeks, a hard hat, and overalls. His floppy brown hair poked out from under his hat, and he had a smile like nothing could bring him down. He waved at me to follow him, and we took each end of the cart, him pulling and me pushing, and headed down the track.

"So, are you liking the mines?" He asked over his shoulder.

"Uh, yeah…I guess," I answered.

"Yeah, I understand if you are not into it right away but do not worry, this job is great once you learn the ropes. I have been here for three years and love every minute."

I narrowed my eyes at his back, wondering if that was his true opinion or if he was skor influenced. I hated that my uncle had made me doubt everyone's motivations and personalities. I looked forward to a day when I did not have to be suspicious about someone's feelings or actions.

"Do you get any skor, you know, to keep?" I asked nonchalantly.

He chuckled and shook his head. "If you are thinking of stealing a piece, I would advise against it. For one, it is not refined so it does not look too good and does not have as much value, and two if a commoner was seen with a piece of unrefined skor they would probably be fined."

I shook my head though he could not see it with his back to me. "No, I mean, have you gotten any as a gift or payment?"

He shook his head again. "No, not yet. However, I heard the new King will be giving everyone in Skorval a piece as a gift to bring in the new reign. Isn't that great?"

"Yeah," I said softly and without any excitement behind it, "great."

"Have you heard what people are saying about the King and his skor?" I asked, trying to get a feel for where his loyalties laid.

He shrugged. "Yeah, I have heard but it sounds like rumors and crazy talk. Magic rocks and a King bent on ruling all the kingdoms?" Torin chuckled. "Silly."

I frowned at his back but now was not the time to argue and show my hand.

"Here we are," Torin announced when we came across the large circular door that led to the storage room.

He took the key from around his neck and inserted it in the lock in the middle of the door. There were no door handles so once he turned the key he pushed against the metal of the door, and we watched as it silently glided open.

He gestured for me to push while he pulled the cart into the room. I glanced behind me and saw the door was left open while we took the cart further in. I noted that as a possible entrance plan for later. Then I took in the room and gasped.

Torin chuckled knowingly and guided our cart to an empty space in the middle of the room. "We have to leave it here for processing which the team in charge of that will do first thing tomorrow morning," he explained.

I did not acknowledge his statement and instead turned around to see everything, cataloguing it all to report to my friends later. There was one thing I realized fast. We would not be able to destroy the stockpile of stones without bringing the whole mountain down.

The room was huge, and every wall of the circular area was covered in mountains of blueish-green stones, unrefined, some large, some the size of a fingernail. Carts laid about holding more stones. It looked like Sorden could let everyone in the mountain take a year's vacation and put the mine on hold and still have enough stones leftover when they got back.

A hole in the ceiling drew my attention and I pointed to it. "What is that for?" I asked Torin.

He turned to me then followed my finger to where I pointed. He tilted his head at it then shrugged. "Ventilation?"

He did not seem to care that there was a hole and went back to locking the cart in place. I drifted over to the spot below the hole and looked up, but I could only see darkness. Where did it lead? It seemed irresponsible to have this place locked only to have an opening in the ceiling for someone to use. It was not small either. A whole cart could fit through it.

Torin called to me, so I did not get to inspect the hole further. I gave it one last studying look before following Torin out. He dragged the door shut using the edge and quickly removed his fingers before they got crushed. Then he used the key around his neck to lock it and smiled at me.

"Mission accomplished."

We headed back along the tracks, him immediately launching into stories of his time here while he kept pace with my quick steps as I tried to hurry so I could see if Jasta found anything. I tuned him out, only nodding or humming interest every so often to make him think I was hanging onto every word.

Finally, we reached the room where we had met, and he lifted his key for me to see. "Well, I better get this back to your Overseer. It was nice meeting you and I appreciated the help."

I nodded and gave him a wave then made my way out of the mines before he could try telling me another story.

The fresh air hit me in the face when I got outside and I breathed in a deep lungful of it, only now realizing how stale and musty it was in the mines. I took another breath but as I let it out and was about to turn to go find the tents and my friends, a cold piece of metal poked me in the back, and someone said quietly but forcefully, "Stay right there, and put'em up."

Chapter 10

-Kip-

"Wake up."

I shook Barent's shoulder until his eye cracked open then stepped back so I was not crowding him.

"If you are still willing to join me, then we should leave now."

Barent sat up, one eye squeezed shut and his other only partially open as he looked around and took in his surroundings. Then he studied me and seemed to remember everything we discussed last night. Both eyes opened wide, and he nodded with a determined expression. "I wish to join you still."

He stood up and started to stretch.

There was nothing to gather since we fled without a bag or provisions. Which reminded me. I took out the medicine the apothecary gave me and took my dose. The other medicine would need water so I would have to wait until I could refill my canteen at a running water source to take it.

I turned to Barent after stashing the pills away in a pocket. "We will need to find food and water soon, but for now let us head toward Skorval."

Barent nodded his agreement, and we left the safety of the trees to the road. There did not seem to be any guards or villagers searching for us but that could change anytime.

"This way," Barent said, pointing to the right.

The journey took all day. We found an apple tree on the way and ate our fill in fruit, but water was still elusive. There were some people heading in the opposite direction, toward the village far behind us occasionally and I tilted my hat over my eyes so it would be harder to recognize me, but we were not worried about them knowing us both as escapees. Near evening, just before the sun started to set did we see the upward trail that led to the first mountain of Skorval. We had seen the mountain from a distance and had used it as a guiding point but now we were there, at the mountain.

Barent looked to me then up the trail. "What do we do once we get there? How will you find your crew? That is if they are there roaming around and not captured."

"Well, knowing Ana and the others, I would expect them to divide and conquer. So, I would say there are some in the town, some in the mines, and some in the palace. I do not know how many they recruited to help them, but I know they are resourceful and would be trying to take down the King and his trade in any way possible." I clapped Barent on the shoulder. "Ready to make some trouble?"

He gave me a nervous smile but nodded. Together we followed the trail up to the first platform. I had not been to Skorval since my parents were alive but not much had changed in the way of getting access to the place. Skorval was surrounded by three mountains. One access point was from the ocean in the east and these platforms in the southwest since the trails cut off every so often. The northern mountain was impenetrable, so Skorval was the safest place in Shayd.

The platform would be our first test. A guard controlled access to it and therefore access to Skorval. If he recognized me then it would be a lot more difficult to get in. We would need to climb around, and my ribs were still quite sore and not ready for that kind of exertion.

I took my coat off and handed it to Barent who took it with a perplexed expression.

"You lead the way," I said, and took a step back. "Our story is that we are visiting a family friend in the outer ring."

They were looking for one man in a long coat and tri-pointed hat, not two men with one of each. I was hoping the guards would not look too closely. I also unstrapped my sword and gave it to him to carry so he could hide it beneath the coat. His eyes widened a bit but I nudged him forward and kept a step behind him the whole time, using his body to shield me for the most part.

The guard at the platform watched us approach and placed his hand on his sword pommel by his side. Barent tensed but I placed my hand on his back which made him relax.

"State your business?" The guard said.

Barent repeated my lie. "We are visiting a family friend in the outer ring."

He studied Barent, taking note of the coat then leaned around him to peer at me. I smiled confidently at him but kept my hat low. Seeming to pass inspection the guard stepped aside and swept his hand out to the platform.

"Stay in the middle unless you want to fall to your death, in which case, Skorval is not liable for your idiocy," he said and moved to a rope and gear system that would pull us to the next trail.

We did as he said and a moment later, the platform lurched and we had to brace our feet shoulder width apart to keep from falling over.

The ride up was swift and soon we were stepping off onto another dirt path. We continued this all the way up and down the other side until the last platform let us off onto a cobbled path instead of dirt that would lead into town and branch off along the way to the different rings.

When we were out of sight of the guards, Barent tried handing my coat and sword back, but I held up my hand to fend him off. There would surely be more guards around and until I could find a satchel to hide my hat or coat in then he would have to keep it.

"Where to first?" Barent asked when we reached our first crossroads.

"We continue forward. Into town for now. Then if we do not find anyone, we will go up to the mines where I am sure one of my crew will be."

"Can we get some food first?" Barent asked and as if it was a signal, both of our stomachs growled their displeasure.

We chuckled at the sounds.

When the growling was done, I patted my belly and nodded. "Food first."

The closer we got to the center ring, the more people we saw and the more crowds we had to maneuver through. No one gave us any mind so long as we did not bump into them. Shops lined each side of the street, mostly furniture or clothing so we continued until we found the first shop with food in it.

Barent spotted it at the same time and we both picked up our pace until we were practically salivating at the door to the shop. The sign overhead read 'Granny's' and the smell coming from inside as well as the breads on display in the window told me it was a bakery.

"Well, are you going to come in or stand there letting all the bugs in?" An old woman asked from behind the counter.

"My apologies," I said and stepped into the shop, pushing Barent ahead since he was standing in front of me.

We approached the counter where the woman was waiting. Barent shifted to look at the baked goods in the display case.

"What do you recommend?" I asked.

"I just made some fresh bread. I could make you a sandwich. I also have stew I could put in a bread bowl."

My eyes lit up at the stew suggestion and my stomach rumbled in response. "Stew please. Make that two." I gestured to Barent who popped back over at my words.

"Could we also get some tea please?" Barent asked.

The old woman winced and looked behind her. Then she turned back to us and nodded once. "There is a water shortage right now. I had to get mine from the river near my house in the third ring, but for the two of you I think I can spare some to make a pot of tea."

"Water shortage?" asked Barent.

She waved her hand in the air and frowned. "Oh, yes, some rebels blew up our water station yesterday. Left us with only one spout to pull from. It has been chaos there since."

She started moving around, preparing our order.

We sat at a table nearby to wait.

Barent sat forward crossing his arms on the table and whispered, "Was that your crew that did that to the water station?"

I looked around to make sure we were not overheard then nodded. "Sorden has a way of drugging the water. It gets in your head and messes with your will."

Barent's eyes widened and he started to stand. "Then we have to warn her. We can't drink the tea, no one should."

I reached across the table and pulled him back into his seat. "It is fine. She said she is getting her water from a river. Moving water does not work very well, if at all. We can drink the tea."

That seemed to calm him then he sat forward again. "But we have to warn her and the others here." He glanced at the couple sitting on the other side of the cafe.

"I am sure my crew has already thought of it but even if they or you tell others the truth, the skor is too strong and not everyone will believe."

Barent sat back. "I realize now how difficult this all must be for you."

The owner carried over two plates, a round piece of bread with stew inside on them, and set them down in front of us before going back to grab the tea. By the time she came back with it, Barent and I were already partially through our meal.

She chuckled and placed the tea down. "If you need anything else, just call for me. People call me Granny." She left us to finish her work behind the counter leaving us alone with the delicious food.

When we were done, we both sat back and patted our bellies.

"That was probably the best meal I have ever had," Barent said.

I laughed. "Is it the best because it is the only thing you have had to eat in two days or because it is cooked to perfection?"

"Can't it be both?"

We laughed and started to rise.

"Captain?" a shocked voice rang out, freezing me in place.

We looked over to see who recognized me, ready to fight our way out if necessary, but when I saw who it was I half laughed-half choked on a sob and stumbled over to my friend who had just walked into the shop.

I wrapped my arms around her and squeezed her tight.

Her head only came up to my sternum so when she tried speaking, all I heard were mumbles and felt the rumble against my chest.

She tapped my back frantically, so I let go. She dramatically drew in a deep breath and patted her chest. "You come back from the dead and the first thing you do upon seeing me is suffocate me to death."

I laughed and Gesebe's dramatics turned into something softer as she smiled at me with tears glistening in her eyes.

"Gesebe. It is good to see you, but I did not expect you to be here."

That brought an instant frown to her face and she put her hands on her hips. "Of course, I am here. Both me and Brenev."

My eyebrows rose at that news and I looked around for Gesebe's husband. She waved away my searching gaze. "He is at the docks." A flicker of worry entered her eyes, pulling her brows down but it was quickly replaced by anger. She slapped me on my arm and scolded me. "Why did you scare us like that? You could have told us you were alive. They told me you fell off a cliff. We thought you died." It was her turn to hug me tight.

"I thought I did too."

We stared at each other in wonder of the other's presence until Barent cleared his throat behind me to get our attention.

I turned to him and Gesebe peered around me at the stranger with distrust.

He looked between us nervously and raised a hand in greeting. "Hello. I'm Barent. His Highness's newest recruit."

Gesebe quickly looked around then moved forward and pulled Barent's hand down and tugged him to one of the tables.

"Shh," she scolded, "you cannot just throw that title around in public. Not right now."

Barent paled and looked around, realizing his mistake. I followed them and we settled in at the table.

Gesebe glowered at Barent. "Go order me some food."

Barent looked to me and raised his brows, silently asking if she was serious.

"Please," I said more politely than the Councilwoman.

Barent got up and went to the counter to order from Granny.

"He is a good man," I said, hinting that she should be nice.

She shrugged.

We sat there a moment, silent once again.

Finally, I asked, "Where are the others?"

Gesebe looked around the room again to make sure no one was listening. The couple at the other end of the bakery had not paid us any attention before and did not seem to be interested now either.

She leaned forward anyway and whispered, "We have people all throughout the rings trying to spread the word. We have Oskai, Edrah, and Edsen infiltrating the castle with some rebels. And we have Lenman, Jasta, and Ren in the mines with some rebels."

"A-and what about Ana? Is she…ok?"

I thought back to our fight on the bridge and only now realized something terrible could have happened to her too. Up to now, I imagined that she survived and got to safety but with Gesebe leaving her out of the report I was starting to think maybe she had not made it. That thought sent panic through me and I started tapping my foot furiously.

Gesebe frowned and looked to the side. "She left me here to go find Jasta in the mines."

Her words sent a wave of relief through me. I puffed out a deep breath and sat back. "So, she is ok. I am glad."

"Yeah, she is ok," Gesebe grumbled then looked at me and must have seen something on my face because her features softened and she spoke to me in a gentle tone. "She was heartbroken. Could not function for a few days. That is until Ren convinced her we needed to move on and complete the mission. But even now when you are mentioned she gets this far away, haunted look." Gesebe shook her head sadly. Then she brightened and slapped me on my forearm. "But she will be glad to see you, everyone will!"

Barent came back with a cup of tea and placed it in front of Gesebe. "Granny will bring over your food in a minute," he told her then he looked to me as he sat down. "What did I miss?"

Chapter 11

-Ana-

I reacted on instinct and dove forward into a roll then popped back up and turned to face my opponent. I dropped my hands that I had raised in defense when I saw who had come up behind me.

"Ha, ha, very funny," I said sarcastically.

Jasta lowered her sword and chuckled. "It is always good to test the Saya's reflexes."

I snorted and nodded toward the mountain with the palace. "I do not think I am Saya anymore."

Jasta came over and placed a hand on my shoulder and waited until I was looking at her to say, "You will always be Saya to me. Now come. Let us go find the others and I will tell you what I found."

Jasta led me to the two tents they were using. Lenman and Ren were sharing one, leaving Jasta with her own, until now. We pushed into the men's tent and the four of us sat with our legs crossed in a circle. It was cramped but we made do.

Ren gestured to me but looked at Jasta when he said, "As you can see, we have a new addition."

Jasta arched a brow at me. "Yes, I see that. And I am sure she will tell me why she is here but first it is my turn."

We leaned in even though we could hear her perfectly in the small space.

"I think I found it."

Ren sat back and let out a surprised laugh. Lenman grinned and patted her on the shoulder. I smiled but reserved my excitement until I knew everything.

"That was fast. How did you find it?" I asked.

"I knew it was on the second level and from there I just had to search each passageway until something familiar stood out. It took a little longer than I hoped because I had stumbled upon it by accident last time and the subsequent events were frantic."

I nodded, remembering her story about Lord Sorden trying to kill her after finding her in his lab then practically chasing her off the mountains and out of Skorval.

She grinned. "But then I found a hidden offshoot to one of the tunnels and a rock door that was almost indistinguishable from the rest of the rock around it…" she looked at each of us, drawing out her story, "except there was a keyhole in the rock."

Lenman raised his hand as if waiting to be called on. "I can probably get us in. I would have to see the lock for myself and picking locks is usually Oskai's area of expertise, but I know a few things."

"You once said that you accidentally walked in and that is how you found it. You never mentioned a lock before," I pointed out.

Jasta nodded and picked at the blanket underneath her. "He must have installed it after I left. Couldn't have any more people stumbling upon his greatest secret now, could he?"

I thought the same but now it left us with the difficulty of getting in. "Tomorrow, we can check it out."

Ren chuckled and jokingly said to me, "But Ana, the Overseer will be very upset if you are late again."

I smacked him in the arm which sent us all laughing.

"If that is all, I think I will retire to another tent." I raised my brows at Jasta, signaling to her that it was time for her to show me her tent.

We left the men and turned into the tent on the left of theirs for the night. We laid down but I spent the next few minutes explaining what I was doing there and what we had surmised of Sorden's plans.

When I was finished, Jasta let out a long breath. "After we are done here, we should go to the palace."

"Agreed."

I wondered if Shula got back to Gesebe yet. I could only hope Gesebe was doing well on her own until then.

The next morning, we got up earlier than needed by two hours, hoping it would be enough time to check out the lab door then get to our assignments. None of us could risk getting fired and kicked off the mountain before we were ready.

Jasta led the way, with Lenman following right behind her then me then Ren. She took us to the second level which could be accessed by a steep trail on the side of the mountain. Thankfully my uncle took precautions and installed a sturdy railing on the outer edge of the trail.

At the second level, Jasta guided us to the third tunnel and swiftly took us to the next one and on. We all stayed quiet, even though there should not be anyone in there. Better safe than sorry.

It was dark in the mines, the sun barely reaching the horizon when we started and the lamps had not been relit yet along the passageways. Our only source of light was a glowing stick Lenman held aloft.

After a few minutes, Jasta pointed to her left and disappeared. I blinked a couple times trying to understand what I had just seen. Ren and I shared a bewildered look and Lenman leaned forward and brought the light closer to the rocks to try to figure out what happened.

Jasta's head reappeared, and I stumbled back. Ren caught me and set me back upright. I gave him a quick grateful smile than focused on Jasta again.

"What are you waiting for? Come on," she whispered.

Lenman stepped forward then sucked in a breath when he saw whatever it was Jasta was talking about then he too disappeared. It was my turn.

I could see the light from Lenman's glowing stick still so I knew they were still there, I just could not see them. I walked toward it and when I got close enough, I noticed it was another tunnel nearly invisible from the rest of the path. No lamps were hung near it so no one would be able to see it even if they were lit. It was barely big enough for one person and angled in a way that you would have to know what you were looking for to find it. How did Jasta accidentally find this? However it was done, we should be grateful it happened, even if it led to her banishment. Something I would be rectifying when this was all over.

We followed slower than before until Jasta suddenly stopped and urged us back a few steps. She backtracked then stared at a piece of wall. I opened my mouth to ask what was wrong when I saw the faint lines in the rock. At first it looked like a natural fissure but on closer inspection the lines made a perfect rectangle the size of a door. Jasta placed her hand in the middle of it and pushed but it did not budge. She then pointed to the cause. Lenman took her place and held the glowing stick close to the lock.

It was similar to the one that led to the storage room, same design and metal but it was smaller and disguised to look like the rock around it.

Lenman pulled some small tools from a pouch on his belt, knelt to one knee to be on level with the lock, and started fiddling with it. We circled around him, unintentionally forming a barrier between him and anyone else who may happen to find us. Not that it was likely. We practically held our breath as we waited for results.

After a couple of minutes one of the tools snapped and Lenman cursed under his breath. He stood up to his full height and put the tools away. He turned to us with a grim look and a shake of his head.

My shoulders slumped and I took one last look at the lock before nodding my head toward the exit. "We should get out of here and think of a new plan."

We turned to go but heard a noise from the other side of the wall, near the door. We all froze. Jasta and I shared a wide-eyed look before ushering the men to hurry. We scrambled out of the small, hidden passageway and hid among the shadows on the other side. Another minute passed before we felt safe to move.

I got close to Ren and whispered in his ear, "You and Lenman go back to the tents, make a cover story for me, and send a message to the palace team to look for a key, Jasta and I will stay here to watch the door." I leaned back to look into his face and waited for his confirmation.

He nodded and gave me a quick hug before tugging Lenman by the sleeve to follow him. I laid my hand on Jasta's shoulder to keep her in place. Lenman looked back at Jasta and tossed her something then gave her a nod before they disappeared down the tunnel.

I looked down at her hand to see a clear stick like the one he held but this one was not lit. As the men disappeared, so did their light.

"We cannot stay here for long," Jasta whispered in my ear.

"My guess is whoever is in that room will not stay there for long, or else they would risk being seen by others," I whispered back.

Jasta cracked the light stick and suddenly our little area of the tunnel was filled with blue colored light. She quickly smothered its intensity under her sleeve but enough light still shown that we could see each other's faces but not much else.

I held up five fingers near the light.

Understanding that I meant we will stay for five minutes, Jasta nodded and leaned back against the wall to wait.

The darkness and the silence began to grate on my senses as we waited despite the faint light coming from Jasta's sleeve. I wished to take out the glowing stick and brighten everything up more. The darkness was starting to press in on me and give me the feeling of being stuck in a small space. I reached out and squeezed Jasta's hand.

Jasta held up one finger to let me know we would leave in one minute. I nodded and tried to keep my breathing calm.

Just then a slight scrape of stone against stone sounded in the quiet. I perked up and squeezed her hand in warning this time. I tugged her closer until we were pressed against the opposite wall and, knowing what to do, Jasta covered the light until almost nothing could be seen now.

I peeked around the corner, into the offshoot of the tunnel. My eyes widened when I saw my uncle, the new King of Shayd, only ten feet away. He held a lit lamp that illuminated his classic maroon coat and the doorway in front of him. From my angle I could not see inside, and he closed it before I could attempt to do more. He produced a key from around his neck and locked up his laboratory before tucking the key back into his shirt.

A second later he turned, and I snatched my head back before I could be seen. Jasta tapped on my shoulder, but I ignored her.

Footsteps echoed against the stone floor, coming closer. His light bathed the ground the closer he got and we pressed our backs further into the wall as if we could become the stone. Tiny rock points dug into my body through my clothes, and I knew I would have marks on my skin after this.

As long as Sorden continued on to the entrance of the mines we would not be seen but if he decided to head further into the mines he would run straight into us after turning the corner.

We held our breath and soon the light filtered out into the tunnel and Sorden walked away from us and his lab.

Jasta released a breath of relief next to me. I was relieved too but also…

Sudden rage filled my body, unexpected but it should not have been. He was right there. We could end this all now. I lurched forward, ready to snap his neck. Not just for what he did to the people of Shayd, Kip's family, the other royals, and the crew of that Skorval trading ship, but for what he did to Kip too. He had so much to answer for and all of our problems could be ended there.

Jasta yanked me back and I spun on her and wrenched my arm free.

"You cannot kill him here," she whispered in my ear.

"Why not?" I hissed, barely able to keep quiet.

"He probably has a weapon, we do not, so he could hold us off until help arrives. Then when the miners come they will see us, he will get away, and our whole operation will be blown."

"We have the element of surprise, and he is getting farther away so it is now or never."

I jumped away from her before she could grab me again and raced after him as quietly as I could. When I was right behind him, I kicked out at the back of his knee. Sorden cried out in surprise and dropped his lantern as he fell to one knee. I punched out and hit his temple making him fall to both knees, but he did not collapse completely. Like a professional he did not stay down for long. He jumped back up and spun, already having his sword halfway out of its scabbard. I kicked his hand which made him let go of the grip and it slid back into the scabbard. His eyes widened when he realized who was attacking him. Then his lips formed a sly smirk.

"Hello, niece. How is that Captain of yours?" His brows pulled together in false sorrow. "Oh right. Oops." Then he cackled and reached for his blade again.

Shouting out my rage until it filled the tunnel I leapt for him, aiming for his neck with both hands.

If I was in my right mind, I would have gone for the knees then choked him from behind but my anger clouded my judgement. I wrapped my hands around him, cutting off his air, but he continued to smile.

"Ana!"

Jasta tackled me from the side and we both landed in a heap on the ground. The air whooshed from my lungs and pain zinged up and down my arm from where I landed on it.

I sat up and glared at Jasta who jumped up and reached out a hand to help me stand.

When I did not take the offering, she explained, "He was about to stab you."

I glanced behind her, and my eyes widened. I reached out and yanked Jasta down again just as my uncle's blade swung through the spot she had been in.

"Now we are even," I said.

We both rolled to the sides just as his blade came down at us and we popped up to a stand to face him. She was on his left side, and I came to be on his right.

He only took a second to take our new positions in before going for me. He swung at my head then stabbed out at my chest when I dodged it.

Sensing movement behind him, Sorden swung around and blocked a punch from Jasta with his arm then stabbed at her with his sword. She jumped back in time to avoid it and we circled him, looking for a new opening.

"Come now, let us talk about this civilly," Sorden said.

The shadows cast by the lantern on the ground made his features look harsher and his eyes look more menacing.

"The time for talking is over, Uncle," I sneered as I said the familial title. We may have been related by blood, but he was no longer my family. My family were the pirates, my royal friends from the other kingdoms, and the rebels we made along the way.

He huffed and placed a hand on his chest like I hurt him. Then he smirked and held his sword aloft once more. "Do not worry. I have plans for you and soon you will forget about your pirates and rebels."

With that remark he attacked and for the next few minutes Jasta and I tried landing hits whenever there was an opening, but he was good at covering any up quickly.

"Ana, we are about to have company."

I did not register the noise until Jasta's warning. Clangs from mining tools and chatter echoing down the tunnels could be heard over the sound of our fight. That meant we only had a couple minutes to finish this before we had company.

I kicked out at Sorden's knee, but he hopped back and swung at me. Jasta took the opening and kicked the back of his knee behind him which made him fall to one knee. I punched his face then kicked his stomach. Jasta struck his wrist and his sword clattered to the ground. He breathed heavily as he looked up at me but there was no fear.

"Guards! Guards! Rebels in the mines! Guards!" Sorden shouted at the top of his lungs.

Pounding feet suddenly boomed from the ends of each tunnel. Whether they were miners or guards I was not sure, but we could not stick around to find out. Except if we left now, he would still live and then would hunt us down, making our job ten times, no, a hundred times harder.

Jasta pulled my arm, trying to get me to run. I yanked it back and stood over my uncle. He watched us smugly and slowly got back to his feet.

Shouts could be heard now from those approaching us. Sorden answered them. "Over here, hurry!"

Jasta pulled me again.

I started to turn away, but Sorden's comment stopped me.

"If you think that Captain was the last one, wait until I find all of the pirates."

I spun around and before anyone could see it coming, I punched his face so hard his body jerked to the right and collapsed in a heap on the ground. I shook out my hand at the immediate pain, but it was worth it. Too bad we could not stay to do more damage. I saw the lights from the people approaching and this time I let Jasta pull me away, but not before I reached down and grabbed the key from around Sorden's neck.

Chapter 12

-Kip-

The trek up the mountain to the mines was a long one. My ribs and head ached despite having taken some medicine for them that morning. The bottle from the apothecary only had one day of medicine left but the way I was going, reinjuring myself and doing strenuous activities, I may need to stop by a local shop to get a refill. The powder medicine was still half full, and a dose of it was mixed into in my canteen that I was able to fill up before leaving Gesebe. She had a bucket of water that she had carried from a river in one of the outer rings.

"Do you think that Shula person will meet up with Gesebe today?" Barent asked through heavy breaths.

He was not used to climbing up and down mountains even though he lived most his life not too far from one.

"Probably, it has been a couple days. Either way Gesebe can handle herself and the others. She has been doing it for years."

Gesebe had let us stay in the home of one of Ana's elite warriors which doubled as their base of operations currently. I insisted we leave first thing in the morning, so Gesebe was still asleep when we parted.

"Yeah, I picked up on that," Barent chuckled, "but I am still concerned. She looks so…"

"Small? Innocent?" I laughed and shook my head. "Do not let it fool you."

Another few minutes of silence then Barent broke it again with heaving pants. "How much longer?"

It was a good thing he did not have to wear my heavy coat anymore or else he would be soaking in even more sweat and heat. Gesebe had given us a satchel found in Shula's closet. I put my hat and coat in it since they were my most identifiable traits and added some healing water vials, courtesy of Gesebe, and some food. I did not use any water on myself so we would have enough in case of an emergency. I could handle the pain for now.

"Not long."

True to my word, we reached the top after fifteen minutes. I wrapped my arm around my ribs to contain the growing pain and breathed deeply, trying to catch my breath from the trek up. Barent collapsed to the ground even more tired from the walk than me. He suddenly sat up and pointed to the right with a half-tortured exclamation. I followed his finger to the spot he pointed to.

A platform like the ones that brought people up the southwestern mountain into Skorval waited for use.

I should have known they would have one here too. I did not see it below so assumed the workers or visitors all climbed the mountain using the winding trail.

Barent glared at me.

I shook my head and smiled at him. "I swear I did not know."

Barent snorted, disbelieving, then groaned as he took his time to stand up. When we were finally breathing easier, we took our first look around. Three tunnels led into the mines and a dirt path on the left and right led to the levels above.

"Where will we find your crew?" Barent asked.

I shrugged and pointed to the tunnel on the right. "We can wander around until I spot someone I know."

Barent looked up at the other levels then at the other tunnels and shot me a disapproving frown. "We will be here for days then."

I shrugged again and headed toward the right tunnel. He followed but muttered words I could not quite make out under his breath.

The tunnel led to a large circular room. People were either talking to each other over maps and tools, hacking at the walls with pickaxes, or loading up the cart in the middle. No one paid us any attention, so we kept going after a quick look around. The farther into the mountain we went the more tunnels branched off and we had to make quick decisions on which to take. So far there was no one I recognized. I assumed my crew picked up some people from the Shayd mines and other towns that we met along the way to help the rebellion here in Skorval, but I did not see any of them either.

After a while, Barent placed his hand on my arm to stop me. We huddled against a darkened wall to talk but I kept my eyes searching around me for someone I knew.

"We cannot keep going like this. We will be here forever. I have an idea."

I finally looked at him. "What idea?"

"Ask one of the Overseers."

I looked at him incredulously. What were we going to say? Hi, do you know where a group of rebels might be?

"Trust me," he said and walked to the middle of the third circular room we had found.

I shook my head but followed after him.

The Overseer of this area was standing next to the cart of skor with a clipboard and glanced up at us when we got close. He squinted at our apparel and looked around the room before landing back on us. "Where are you supposed to be? I do not recognize you."

Barent pasted on a bright smile. "My thoughts exactly. You see, we are a little lost. We were looking for the area where new recruits go."

Suddenly I understood what Barent's idea was. My crew and any they brought with them would be considered new recruits and need training. If they had not already been spread out after their instruction, then that group was where we would find them.

The Overseer, a young man with crinkle lines around his eyes smiled and shook his head. "You are way off target if that is what you are looking for." He used his clipboard to point to the left. "You need to go to the far-left tunnel to the first chamber. They should be in there."

Barent waved a thank you/goodbye before we backtracked to the entrance then took the left tunnel and followed it to the first chamber as instructed.

This room was quieter than the others and I saw why as soon as I spotted the people. Instead of hacking at the walls or carting around buckets of stones and talking to each other, they were huddled in a group in the back as their Overseer instructed them on something. Barent grinned at me and led the way over to the group. I looked at each person and nearly tripped over my feet when I saw the two tallest in the group. Tlaren and Lenman! Finally!

I searched around them for more familiar faces but only those two stuck out. If Lenman was there, then I knew Jasta would be close by, but I did not see her familiar brown hair with a green ribbon anywhere. We stayed in the back of the group, not wanting to disturb the lesson or draw attention to us. I was surprised no one noticed our late arrival.

Barent leaned close and whispered, "See anyone you know?"

I nodded and his eyes widened. I gestured to the two tallest men in the group and Barent tuned to look. His eyes got even wider if that was possible.

"Is that Prince Tlaren?" he asked awed.

I was surprised he recognized the Prince without the zigzag tattoo. I nodded and shushed him. We waited until the Overseer ended his lesson and everyone dispersed before approaching my friends.

I suddenly felt nervous. They both thought I was dead. What were they going to think when they saw I was not? Maybe we should have found a way to do this elsewhere. I glanced at Barent who nodded at me to go on. I cleared my throat and walked the rest of the way to my friends. They were against one of the walls, halfheartedly hacking away at the rock with their mining tools, but they looked to be in deep conversation.

I tapped Lenman on the back and stepped back next to Barent. They both turned and looked at the both of us. A second passed before recognition lighted both their faces. Their eyes widened and they glanced at each other then back to me. Their eyes briefly flitted to Barent but quickly dismissed him as they came back to look at the ghost in their presence.

Ren reached out a finger and poked me in the cheek then gasped.

I swatted his hand away and chuckled. "I am real."

Lenman cursed and suddenly folded me into a tight hug. He was much taller than I was so I now felt what

Gesebe had when I hugged her. I tried speaking but my words came out mumbled since my face was pressed into his chest. Lenman pulled back and let out a surprised laugh then shook me by the shoulders.

"You're here. You are really here!" He said a little too loudly.

"Shh." I looked around to see if anyone heard him. Only a couple people glanced at us and shook their heads before going back to their jobs. Thankfully the Overseer was across the room and had not yelled at us yet.

Ren's eyes teared up which made my own mist in response.

"Oh my, I do not think I have ever seen a Prince cry, let alone two."

Barent's voice broke up our reunion. I turned to him and punched him in the shoulder. "I was not crying."

Barent raised an eyebrow at me but did not contradict my words.

"Who's this?" Lenman asked eyeing Barent warily.

"What happened to you?" Ren asked at the same time.

I rubbed my ribs and sighed. "I will tell you," I said, answering both of them, "but first where are Jasta and Ana?"

Lenman and Ren looked at one another.

"What?" I asked, seeing the silent communication but not understanding it.

Ren rubbed the back of his head. "You just missed them."

I frowned and waited for him to elaborate.

Lenman was the one to continue. "We found the location of the laboratory this morning. We got separated and they ran into Sorden."

They shared a look again.

Panic and worry started to take root and I stepped closer and gripped each of them by their arm. "Where are they? Are they in trouble?"

Ren tilted his head side to side. "In a way, we all are." Seeing my impatience, Ren removed my hand from his and squeezed it reassuringly. "Do not worry too much. They knocked him out and stole his key. Ana is on her way to the palace to warn the others. Jasta escorted her down the mountain."

"If they were going down when we came up, how did we miss them?" Barent asked. Then he shook his finger in the air as realization came.

At the same time, Barent and I said, "The platform."

I sighed and shook my head. We were so close yet...

"We are planning to look into the laboratory when Jasta comes back," Lenman explained.

I nodded. "Good, we will join you."

Lenman raised a brow and put a hand on his hip. "Again, who is this?

I gestured to Barent. "He is joining us. He helped me out in a tough situation on my way here."

Barent stretched out a hand. "I'm Barent."

Ren and Lenman looked at the hand but neither reached out to take it. They pointedly ignored the outstretched hand and turned to me.

"How exactly are you here right now?" Lenman asked, circling back to the fact that I was alive and present.

I sighed. "It is a long story. I would prefer to tell you once Jasta arrives, so I do not have to repeat myself."

Ren and Lenman shared a look again. Coming to some kind of silent agreement, Lenman put his arm around my shoulders and guided me away. "Then I think we should take this outside. She might get…emotional."

Ren looked around to make sure we were not noticed as we left through the tunnels back to the entrance. He veered right once the light of day surrounded us and we were out of the mines. Lenman continued to keep his arm around my shoulder and Barent followed behind. Soon we were at a set of tents that all looked the same. It reminded me of the white miner's tents at the Shayd mines.

Ren stopped and looked back over his shoulder to Lenman. "Maybe you should go wait for her."

Lenman nodded and released me. He patted me on the back and gave me a smile before heading back to the tunnels to wait for Jasta. Barent and I continued on when Ren gestured to follow him. Eventually he stopped at a tent that had no identifiable markings on it but somehow he knew it was his. He opened the flap and gestured for us to go first.

The space was small. When the three of us sat down, our legs brushed each other and our belongings filled the rest of the space. We would have to take it outside when the others arrived.

Ren reached behind him and took out a couple apples and handed them to us before reaching back and grabbing another for himself.

"So, what do you remember?" Ren asked, suddenly nervous. He would not meet my eyes and picked at his apple, creating half-moons in the skin with his thumb nail.

I remembered everything. The Shayd mines. The well. The kiss. The fight. Ren. The bridge. The fall.

"I do not blame you."

Ren's eyes snapped up to meet mine and I could see them shimmering as tears threatened to fall. "How could you say that? It was my fault."

I reached out and laid a hand on his forearm. "No, it was Sorden's."

"What is he talking about?" Barent asked softly.

We looked to him then at each other. Ren was the one to answer. "I betrayed my friends when it mattered. It resulted in his death…well almost death."

I shook my head vehemently. "It was *not* your fault," I told him again then turned to Barent to explain further, "I have not exactly told you everything about Sorden's control. He has been manipulating people with skor. He is a known alchemist and has done something to the stones. He also found a way to turn it to powder and drug liquid. He slipped some to the Kings and Queens during the coronation ceremony. Ren was not in his right mind."

Barent looked between us with wide eyes. "Wait, you're telling me those blue rocks that everyone is so crazy about can control minds?"

We nodded.

He shook his head and let out a heavy breath. "And to think I was going to get one for my mother." He blinked as he remembered something we said and frowned. "How did you almost die?"

A dark look passed over Ren's face. I knew then that my words would not fix what he saw as his fault. I would need to find a way to show him.

"There was a fight on a bridge. Sorden cut the ropes and I fell. But as you can *see*," I said emphasizing the last word, "I am perfectly fine."

Ren's eyes scanned me from head to toe, looking for any injuries. I tried to sit straighter and ignore the throbbing in my ribs and slight headache. Fortunately, those were not visible.

Barent was cut off from asking more questions when the tent flaps opened.

"She is here," Lenman said and left, dropping the flaps back over the entrance.

Chapter 13

-Ana-

Yes, I made a mistake.

Now I would have to speed up our plans.

Once Jasta bid me farewell at the bottom of the mountain I made my way across the outer ring of Skorval and up the eastern mountain to the palace. The trail going up to my home was a familiar one, but it also gave me homesick pains. What I would give to be training in the yard with my elite warriors or relaxing in my rooms with a nice hot tea. But I could do all that once we fixed the problems going on in Skorval.

We had left my uncle lying on the ground for the miners to find and scrambled out of there. I knew the next step was to go to the palace and warn the rebels there and try to get the Kings and Queens out before Sorden could call the guards. By now, I was only a few hours ahead of him. It would be a tight window, but we would have to make do.

My legs burned by the time I reached the palace. Getting across Skorval without a horse was much more difficult, especially if I was rushing the entire way by running or speed walking. The uphill walk along a winding trail did not help either. I could not risk taking the platforms in case someone recognized me.

At the palace gates, there were guards stationed but I grew up there and knew the back ways into it, although it would take a bit of climbing. I skirted around the gates to the edge of the mountain where it dropped off into craggy rock faces and the land below. The sight of the ocean froze me in place and a sense of home came over me. I gazed out across the water and breathed in the salty air. That was the good stuff.

Focusing back on my goal, I started my climb out across the rocks and up the mountain to where I knew my rooms to be.

The climb was one I had done many times, usually unnecessary but I liked the challenge. Thankfully it paid off and I was able to get up to the balcony of my rooms easily. Once on the balcony, I tried the doors that led inside but they were locked. I hated to ruin the beautiful handmade glass brought in from Farlo but it was the only way in. Closing my eyes, I used the pommel of one of my blades to smash the glass door. The raining debris made quite a bit of noise and I froze, waiting to see if someone would come investigate.

After a minute of silence, I crept across the door frame, careful of the glass around me and finally I was inside the palace. It had been weeks since I was there last, but everything was the same. The maids had apparently continued to clean it because the bed was made and not a speck of dust could be found.

Now would be the tough part: going about the place and not being recognized. I walked to my closet and rifled through the clothes inside. There were not many since I preferred to dress in the same uniform as the other elite warriors—black pants, black shirt, red jacket, and braided hair. The hair at least I could change. No one there had seen it down except maybe the night maids.

I made quick work of undoing the braid I had assembled that morning and let my raven hair fall across my back. The hair was wavy since it had been tied in a braid for so long. I found a pair of yellow and green colored pants and matching shirt, bought by my uncle in Drisl while hoping I would dress more like the heir I was rather than a Saya of warriors. I had reminded him my heir status was supposed to be secret and he had relented. The material was smooth, light, and flowy—common elements in Drislian clothing. I never wore the clothes before, which would be perfect for disguising myself now.

Once I felt confident enough I would not be easily recognized I slipped out of my rooms and headed down the hall for the staff quarters. I had no idea where the rebels would be, but I assumed many of them would be playing the role of common staff since everyone knew the common staff were the eyes and ears of palaces. It was midday, so many if not all would be about doing their jobs. I did not have much hope of finding my friends, but it was as good a start as any.

A few people eyed me curiously on the way, but none stopped to ask who I was or what I was doing. There were guards patrolling the halls, but none seemed like they were alerted to the possible presence of rebels. Which meant my uncle had not gotten back yet and had not sent a message ahead.

I reached the staff quarters and began peeking my head into each room. The rooms were small with one bed and a couple other pieces of furniture in each one.

Some had personal items hung on walls or placed around the room but it was mostly simple. It was not hard to do a quick search of each room from the doorway and after a few I was starting to assume no one was in that part of the palace.

"Can I help you?"

Or maybe I was wrong.

I turned to see a young woman holding a pitcher of what I assumed was water. I did not know where she came from or where she was headed but I could use the opportunity to find where the others were.

"Hello, yes, I was looking for someone. Do you know where the new staff would be?"

She looked me over, probably trying to figure out if I was a lady of the palace or a new staff member who got lost.

After a moment, she nodded her head forward, indicating the direction behind me. "Some are in the kitchen and some are in the upstairs rooms. A few might be in the garden and main hall, but most new staff start in the kitchen and rooms." She looked me over one last time but decided I was harmless enough and moved on down the hall in the direction she had indicated.

"Thank you," I called after her.

That barely narrowed it down but I only needed one familiar rebel face to find the rest so I would start with the kitchen. Unfortunately, that was one place I was familiar with which meant someone was likely to recognize me.

I sighed and walked confidently to the kitchen making sure to look like I belonged by keeping my eyes straight ahead and walking quickly as staff often did around there. If I was called out on the way then I would deal with it then. However, I made it all the way to the kitchen without any incident. I knew from experience my luck could not last much longer.

I pushed the door open enough to peek inside. People in aprons and hats bustled about preparing the next meal for the palace folk. My stomach grumbled at the smells wafting toward me. I had not eaten all day and my stomach was starting to clench because of it.

From that angle I did not see anyone I recognized from the rebel group, but I did see the head chef, Dede, and she would surely recognize me. I let the door close so I could think of a plan.

When nothing came to mind, I decided to risk it, only for a moment. I pushed the doors to the kitchen open and popped inside. I stuck to the outer edges, staying out of the cooks' way as I looked at every face for a rebel. Thankfully they were too busy to pay me any mind. My mouth watered when someone passed by with a pan of steaming buns. I had to force myself not to follow and focused on my task again. I made it nearly all the way around and was almost to the doors again when someone shouted, freezing me in place.

"Stop right there! What are you doing in here?"

Since I was the only one not supposed to be there, I figured they were talking to me and slowly turned around to face them. The cooks did not stop what they were doing but a few looked in my direction confirming they meant me.

Dede was standing a couple feet away with one hand on her hip and a ladle in the other. I knew from experience she liked using that ladle to swat intruders away from the food.

"Hello, Head Chef. My apologies for the intrusion. I was looking for someone."

Her eyes widened in recognition, and she placed a hand over her heart. "Oh my, it's you."

That turned a few more heads in my direction.

I gulped and looked toward the doors. Technically I could fight my way through them but that would draw unnecessary attention and be rude.

"Yes, I am back. But—"

"I have heard things you know," she eyed me warily.

"I am sure you have, but I do not think it is the truth."

She arched a brow at me. "Not true, huh? So you are not the heir then?"

I shrugged and tilted my head. "Well, technically yes, but—"

"And you did not join a group of pirates?"

I opened my mouth but ended up shrugging instead.

"And you have not been giving King Sorden grief?"

At that I frowned and crossed my arms. "Well, yes, and I would do it all again."

I heard a few gasps which made Dede turn in a circle waving her ladle in the air. "Get back to work."

Once the cooks had their heads down and turned away from us, she stalked over to me and waved her ladle. I flinched, assuming she was going to hit me with it, but she only used it as a pointer. "Follow me."

I looked toward the doors, wondering if I could make a run for it and escape before she could call the guards.

Dede snorted. "I am not going to turn you in, now come, girl."

I hesitated for one more moment then followed her. I had always known her to be honest and if she said she would not turn me in then I believed her.

There was a little office attached to the kitchen for the Head Chef to get orders placed and paperwork done. Since most of her time was in the kitchen though, the office was small, barely big enough for two people. She sat at the chair behind her desk then gestured to a stool in front of me.

I sat, but kept my legs slightly pointed toward the door so I could make a run for it if need be.

"I am going to get right to it," Dede said and rested her elbows on the desk as she leaned forward. "I know why you are here. Your little crew and I had a chat a couple days ago."

I frowned and tilted my head, not quite understanding what she meant. Did she think she talked to the rebels assigned to the castle or the elite women warriors?

"I am afraid I do not know what you mean," I said innocently. I wanted to fold my arms, but I knew that was a defensive posture that she would see right through. It never worked in the past when I lied about sneaking food and it would not work now.

She circled the top of her head with a finger. "The bald man?"

I arched a brow. Did she mean Oskai?

"And the brother and sister. They did not say they were related but I knew. It's in the eyes and hair."

Ok, now she meant Edrah and Edsen. She was definitely talking about the rebels then. But I still did not know what they discussed and until I did, I was not admitting anything.

"Hmm. I do not know who you speak of. What did you talk about? Maybe that will help jog my memory."

She knew I knew based on the narrowing of her eyes. I could never hide anything from her.

"I understand your hesitation," she finally said. "They explained everything to me. I thought they were crazy at first. They came in demanding to see the water reserves and advised me to boil it before I used it."

I felt like slapping my forehead. Of course, I should have thought of boiling water. I could have advised the people down in town to do it. Good thinking, palace team.

"So, I did, only because one of them checked in on me and the kitchen every few hours and I did not see any harm in doing it. Then after a couple of days, they explained why they were here and their relation to you." She shook her head and smiled. "I have never left Shayd but I have heard of the Drislian royals. I have even seen the Queen and King around once or twice this week, so I should have known who they were when I first saw them. Especially Princess Edrah with her white-blonde hair, spitting image of her mother."

I brightened after hearing her story. It sounded like the team was able to get the kitchen free of skor influence, and since they fed everyone in the palace that meant everyone here were less likely to be affected too. Brilliant.

"When do you expect to see them again?"

"Around dinner I suppose. I just saw the bald man they were with at lunch a couple hours ago." She gave me a sympathetic smile then brightened. "Stay here until then and I will feed you and you can fill me in on your adventures."

My stomach rumbled and we both laughed.

I spent my time eating fresh baked buns with salted meats and blueberry green tea as I recounted my adventures from when I was first sent on the mission to stop the pirates to our arrival in Shayd, loss in the mines, and plan to end things in Skorval. Dede listened attentively the whole time, sipping on her own tea and occasionally giving orders to the chefs when they popped their heads in.

When I was finished, I slumped on the stool and heaved out a breath. So much had happened in just a few weeks.

"That is certainly much more than your friends told me."

I imagine it would be. My friends did not know her so they would have only told her the bare minimum.

"Yes, and I need to talk to them urgently." Sorden was probably on his way by now if not already there. I have been in the palace for a couple hours and anytime now it would surely go into lockdown until we were found.

Dede pursed her lips and nodded. "I can only imagine how tough this must be. I have always known King—I mean, Lord Sorden to be benevolent but what he has been doing to everyone with that skor, it is just so…disgraceful." She shook her head sadly then stood. "Come on then. One of them should be arriving soon." She paused and turned back to me. Hesitantly she asked, "What are you going to do to him?"

Instant rage filled me and hardened my heart. I felt it twist my face into a look of disgust and fury. I was going to kill him. Looking at Dede though, I knew I could not admit that. I smoothed my face and stood from my stool to follow her out of the small office. "I do not know yet."

She stared at me for a long moment, resignation and sadness pulling her brows and lips down. "I am sure you will do what you know is right."

She left before I could say or do anything.

When we were in the bustling kitchen again, her words from earlier came to mind. "Chef, you said you have seen the Queen and King of Drisl around. Where are they being kept?"

During my story time I told her how the Kings and Queen were in danger and how they had been controlled by Sorden to come and stay at the palace and agree to his whims.

Dede turned to me and tapped her chin. "I think they were in the same hall as Lord Sorden. In those empty rooms he kept."

For as long as I had known him, Sorden kept a whole hall to himself which consisted of about six rooms, a common room, and a balcony garden. Not even I was allowed to stay in the hall and had been given rooms on the floor below his. I thought he liked his privacy but maybe it was paranoia and secrecy. He *had* been cooking up his plot for over thirteen years.

I frowned at her revelation. "I guess it is not that odd. Where else would be better for keeping a tight rein on the royals?"

Dede pursed her lips. "'Tis a shame. They seemed happy enough when I saw them last, nothing to indicate they were here against their will, otherwise I would have helped them much sooner."

"Have you told Princess Edrah and Prince Edsen where their parents are?" If she had, I bet that was where they were now. Trying to free them.

She shook her head then looked down as her cheeks reddened slightly. I was shocked to see the expression on the Head Chef's face because I had never seen her look embarrassed about anything.

"I only just came out of the skor control yesterday evening. They told me their story but had to go as the guards started patrolling. I set them up in some guest rooms. I do not know where they were staying before that." She looked at me apologetically. "I was going to tell them today when I saw them again. Earlier it was only the bald fellow and I wanted to tell the Prince and Princess personally."

I nodded and smiled reassuringly. "No one can blame you for not trusting them when you were influenced by the skor. You were looking out for your King and the other royals."

Dede looked relieved. "They should be here any time now. I have the cooks making them a meal, the same I will be bringing to the other royals. I suspect we could knock two birds with one stone so to say."

"Great idea. It is time to get these royals out."

Chapter 14

-Kip-

"By the stars and sea! You are alive!"

"Shh, you don't want to bring attention to us right now. Need I remind you what happened earlier?" Lenman scolded Jasta.

Jasta ignored him and launched herself at me. I caught her around the waist as she threw her arms around my neck. We hugged like that for a minute or so before she pulled back with tears in her eyes. I set her down and stepped back, smiling.

"Good to see you, Jasta. That was probably the best greeting since Gesebe down in town." I glared at my other friends playfully.

My head snapped back to Jasta when a sharp pain radiated out from my shoulder. Jasta stood there frowning with her hand clenched into a fist leading me to believe she had just punched me.

"What was that for?" I asked, surprised.

"You left us, and made us worry," she said, angrily. "Ana is not the same. You need to tell her you are alive right now."

I looked to Lenman for help but he only shrugged leaving me to deal with her violence alone.

"I came here to find her," I admitted.

She narrowed her eyes and looked me up and down then relaxed. "Are you okay then?"

I nodded though I still had lingering pain from my fall and now her punch. Her lips twisted to the side as she weighed the truth of my words then she nodded accepting my answer.

"Good."

I felt a twinge of guilt not telling them about my still-healing ribs and head but if I did they would coddle me and prevent me from doing what I needed to do.

She swung out without any warning and punched me in the other shoulder.

"Ow! What now?"

"Do not ever scare us like that again."

Ren and Lenman stood to the side of us laughing so I shot them a glare which only made them laugh harder. Barent was looking between us all with wide eyes, unsure what to do.

I rubbed the new pain until it was mostly gone then said, "I heard you found the laboratory." I hoped the new topic would prevent her from inflicting more harm.

Her face brightened. "I did. I was planning on going in as soon as Sorden is gone."

I frowned and rage started to bubble up inside me. "Sorden is here?"

Lenman placed a hand on my shoulder. "Calm down, there is nothing you can do. He is surrounded by miners and a few guards that were called in."

"You have the same look Ana had before she attacked him," Jasta said.

The surprise of that statement pulled me out of my increasing rage long enough to smirk and ask, "Ana attacked him?"

Jasta snorted and Ren chuckled. It was Ren who answered. "She would have killed him if the miners had not shown up."

Lenman added, "That is why she is on her way to the palace. As soon as Sorden starts to move out of here, he will surely sound an alarm and put everyone on guard watching out for rebels."

Jasta nodded, "Which is why we have to destroy that laboratory today."

The three of them looked at each other, determination and anger shining through in the glint in their eyes, pressed lips, and tense stance.

"Ok, then, we wait until he leaves. But can I just point out that it would be so satisfying to end him now?" I said, with a resigned sigh.

Barent squeaked beside me at my violent thought, but the rest of my crew nodded, understanding and agreeing.

It was a couple hours later that we heard noise from the second level entrances. We were still hiding among the tents on the first level on the side of the mine entrances, but we could hear commotion from up above. A second later we heard a voice, familiar and loud, which instantly made my body tense in anger.

"I want everyone on guard and those rebels brought in. I do not care how you do it but find them! Alert the palace!"

Sorden came down the path followed by some guards and an Overseer. The Overseer looked terrified, but the guards had blank looks. Drugged or just obedient?

"Well? What are you still doing here?" He shouted at the guards behind him.

Unperturbed by his outburst, the lead guard said, "My King, you need an escort back."

Sorden frowned and made his way over to the platforms. "Fine. You two," he pointed at the guards in the back, "when we get down there I want you to alert everyone and race ahead to raise the alarm. You two will stay with me," he said pointing at the lead guard and one other.

"What would you like me to do Your Majesty?" The Overseer asked wringing his hands.

Sorden stopped and spun to him making the Overseer squeak and halt abruptly. "Find. The. Rebels." He enunciated each word like the man was an idiot.

I guessed he was showing his true self now. He used to appear benevolent and calm. Now he sounded like what I always knew he was. A tyrant.

Ren and I shared a look and shook our heads before watching the false King again.

"I wish I had a bow and arrow," I said softly. "We could end this now."

"Yeah, too bad Edrah and Edsen are not here, they always seem to have one on them," Ren whispered.

Jasta placed her hand on my back, showing her support. "Do not worry, Captain, we will get him.

Barent looked back and forth between us and the King with a slight furrow between his brows. I did not know if he was confused or angry.

"My niece is probably already at the castle." He felt for something at his neck but growled and stomped off to the platform. "Let us go now."

Jasta chuckled.

"What?" I asked, confused by her behavior.

"He was reaching for his key, but I have it." She dangled the key on a cord in front of me and chuckled again.

I waited until the group was gone and the Overseer went back into the mines before I stood up from where we had been crouched and nodded to the mines above. "Then let us put it to good use."

Jasta led us to the laboratory on the second level of the mines. It was busy as everyone was going about their work, so we had to be careful not to draw much attention, especially since that Overseer was probably alerting the other Overseers to look out for suspicious behavior. I patted the bag at my side that hid my hat and coat. It was a good thing we had it to hide those two distinct items though I would feel more comfortable if I had them on. Ren had to hide his zigzag tattoos with a longer sleeved shirt since they would be recognizable as the Tripscari marks of royalty. At least Jasta got to wear her green ribbon and Lenman could keep on his archer's hood since those were not distinct enough to mark them as rebels or royals.

Something caught Jasta's attention, and she held her hand up for us to halt. Then she disappeared behind the rock wall. Startled, I waited in the tunnel for her to come back out but Lenman pushed me gently forward to follow so I hesitantly stepped forward and that was when I noticed the tunnel split. The offshoot was narrow and very well hidden. I was impressed Jasta had found it those years ago and again recently.

She stopped at a piece of the wall hidden in darkness. The whole hallway there was dark, the only light coming from the lamp in the main tunnel. Lenman cracked a glowing stick and held it out to Jasta who took it and moved it along the rock in front of her, looking for something. After a few seconds she pumped her fist, celebrating her find then gestured me closer. At first it looked like the rest of the rock, but on closer inspection I saw a lock embedded in the wall. Jasta produced the key from a pocket and fit it into the keyhole. She looked at me and grinned.

"Here we go."

Then she turned it and pushed the rock door open creating seams in the wall that were not there before.

Ren and Lenman crowded in behind me, eager for a look into the secret laboratory. I grumbled and pushed them back before going in after her and they followed in right after. Lenman made sure to close the door behind him while the rest of us took our first look of the room. It was a decently large room and nothing like I had seen before. In the middle was a massive table with glass jars of different sizes and shapes, some had green or red liquids in them and were connected by tubes. There was a scale and other measuring equipment. On the left side of the table was a cart like those the miners filled up and on the right was a barrel. I walked closer to inspect the cart and saw it half filled with skor. Suspecting I would find more, I checked the barrel.

I was right that I would find more, it was nearly full, however, it was all submerged in a red hued water. I looked at the equipment again on the table and followed the tubes which ended at one next to the barrel. Sorden must make his mind-altering potion here then coat the skor in it. I wondered if the potion must be used with skor because of some compound in the rocks otherwise Sorden could have used anything and we would never be able to tell. I looked up to see what the others were doing.

Lenman and Jasta were looking over a book laid out on a stand and Ren was looking at something behind some wooden poles in the back of the room. I wandered over to Ren to see what he found. When I was next to him, I saw the wooden poles formed some kind of gate. I tapped Ren to let him know I was behind him though with his warrior training in Tripscari I assumed he already knew.

Ren moved to the side to let me look down at what he found. My brows rose in surprise when I saw a large hole in the ground. I carefully stepped up to the edge and peered down and was surprised again. Down below was a whole other room filled will carts and barrels of skor. Directly below the hole was a wood and metal platform like those that brought people up the mountain.

"This is how he sneaks skor into his laboratory?" I asked mostly to myself, but Ren heard.

"How did no one notice a giant hole in the ceiling of their storage room?" Barent asked. He must have followed me over.

"Did you say hole in the ceiling?" Lenman asked in his deep voice from across the room. How he heard that was a mystery.

We nodded and Lenman left the book to come see what we were talking about for himself. When he took in everything we had, he nodded. "Ana said something about a hole in the ceiling of the storage room this morning. Remember?" He turned to Ren and asked.

Ren nodded.

"Maybe people have noticed the hole but never cared to ask. People have been known to disappear with too much curiosity when it comes to Sorden's affairs." Jasta gestured to herself as proof.

Barent did not know her story but after that hint about her background he widened his eyes. She held the large book they had been looking through in one arm.

"Can we collapse it? It would disrupt the room below and his lab." Ren suggested.

Ren, Jasta, Barent, and I looked at Lenman, our expert in trinkets that blew things up.

Lenman looked in a pouch on his belt, one of many around his waist, then nodded. "I think we can manage that. However, it will cause a great deal of noise and rubble. We will need to be out of here by then."

"Will it destroy the whole room?" Barent asked, a second before I would have.

Lenman shook his head. "Just this part." He waved his hand at the area near the hole and wooden poles.

"Then we should destroy his alchemy set and take anything useful," I said.

Jasta held up the book in her hands. "This has recipes, alchemical recipes. I have not found the recipe for mind controlling skor in here but with time I bet I could."

I gave her a nod. "Good, take that, spread out, and let us get to work."

I had my sword, so I unsheathed it and used it to swing at the materials on the table. Glass shattered and sprayed across the room. Tubes dislodged and spilled green and red liquid on to the table and floor. The red liquid looked darker than it had in the tubes and the puddles of it looked eerily like blood. I shook my head and continued destroying everything in sight.

Lenman grabbed the cart of skor near the table and rolled it to the hole in the ground, his muscles straining at the weight. Ren took care of the barrel at the other end, half carrying-half rolling it to the hole. Barent and Jasta searched the room for more treasures occasionally pocketing things or tossing stuff aside.

We made quick work but when everything was done we stood in a group around the hole and stared down.

"This is it, Sorden will have a hard time recreating his lab. Hopefully that stalls the skor trade and his other plans," Jasta said.

"He still has so much skor already loaded on to ships," Ren pointed out.

They looked to me.

"That is why we have a crew. It is not all up to us. I am sure whoever is in charge of that area of the city will come up with a plan. Who is there?"

Lenman and Jasta looked at one another than to Ren.

Ren scrunched up his face in thought then tilted his head as he answered. "I believe it is Shanm and Cailyn. Other than Gesebe, they were assigned to the town below."

I nodded. "Shanm knows trade and will think about stopping the ships and Cailyn is a good bandit so she will come up with a plan to prevent the ships leaving."

Ren nodded but the others looked unsure. It did not matter, we could not deal with the ships right now.

"We should get moving," I said, turning to the door of the laboratory. "Lenman, deal with the hole."

The others turned to follow but we all froze when we spotted the man in the doorway.

"I thought you closed the door," Barent whispered.

"I did," Lenman stated, throwing the man in the doorway a glare.

"Then how is he here?" Barent asked.

The man held a clipboard in one hand and had his other hand on the rock door. Around his neck was a key on a cord. I looked to Jasta but, knowing what I was thinking, shook her head and held up her key, showing us all she did not leave the key in the lock.

So, there were two keys then.

Chapter 15

-Ana-

Edrah walked through the doors, her hood in place to cover her white-blonde hair, and scanned the room for Dede, her eyes passing over me before sharply coming back to rest on me with recognition. She looked from me to Dede then spoke to someone behind her. Edrah moved into the kitchen and Edsen, her older brother who also wore a hood, and Oskai, Kip's bald bodyguard and trusted Councilman of Under, came in and followed Edrah's pointed finger to me. Their eyes widened but it was Oskai who stalked forward leading the way. Edrah and Edsen slowly followed, keeping an eye on their surroundings. They probably wondered if the others in the kitchen knew who I was and if our cover was blown.

"Ana, what are you doing here?" Oskai whispered when he was close enough. "Did something happen?"

"Ana, you are here. We spoke to your warrior friend the other day. I did not think I would see you so soon." Edrah moved in for a hug which I reciprocated. Edrah gave the best hugs. Well, maybe tied with Ren.

"What are you wearing?" Edsen asked from behind them. He frowned at my yellow clothing.

I scoffed. "It is Drislian. I thought you and Edrah of all people here would appreciate the quality."

Edsen arched a brow at me. "I appreciate the quality, it is the color I disapprove of." He turned to his sister. "We will have to have a talk with the merchants when we get back. That color should be banned."

Edrah rolled her eyes. "It looks pretty. Like a daffodil."

Edsen shook his head but did not argue.

"I have your meals ready," Dede said, directing their attention away from my clothing.

Edrah and Edsen turned away eagerly and followed the head chef to some bowls nearby. Oskai continued to stand by my side. When they were gone, he leaned over and repeated his earlier question. "Did something happen?"

I kept a smile on my face, for those who watched us curiously but whispered in a grave tone. "Our cover is blown. Sorden knows we are here."

Oskai nodded. "I knew this would come eventually. What do you want to do?"

"We need to get the royals out. Now." I appreciated that he did not ask how the cover was blown. I knew it was my fault. If I had not attacked Sorden then we would still be a secret operation. All I could do now was make the best of it and rush the mission. "He will be back soon." It had already been hours since I left the mines. He would surely be on his way by now, alerting the guards as he went. "I also need to send a message to the others to prepare them." I looked at Oskai.

Understanding me, he nodded. "I can get a few of the team in the palace to find the others and warn them. I have an idea, but you might not like it."

I frowned at him. Oskai was one of the few people in our group that I did not have to look up at. He was short compared to Kip, Ren, or Lenman, but next to me and especially Gesebe, he was of average height. "What is it?"

Oskai nodded toward the Drislian siblings. "Let us get them and go somewhere private. This should not be said in public." Oskai looked around warily and touched his waist where I knew his sai were hidden.

Oskai grabbed the other bowl that was laid out for him, gave his thanks to Dede then quietly ushered the siblings out of the kitchen. I followed them, but not before Dede gave me a cart laden with bowls of food for the royals that we could take and use as cover to get into their rooms.

I hid behind Edrah or Edsen when we came upon others. Now that I knew I was still easily recognizable I had to take better care of who saw me.

They led me upstairs, away from the staff quarters and into the main halls of the palace. The cool ocean breezes coming in from the open windows felt nice against my skin. My hair and loose clothing swayed when particularly strong breezes touched me. The smell of the ocean was more prominent with those stronger winds, and I inhaled the familiar scent each time, letting it soothe me even if it was just for a moment.

"Here we are," Oskai announced after we left the open halls to a quieter and more secluded hall of rooms.

Those rooms were used for guests and Dede said she set them up in their own room which would be the last thing my uncle would expect so it seemed a good enough place to discuss business. The guest room was smaller than my own rooms, but they still had a couch and personal bathroom. The bed was smaller, and it looked like at least one of them slept on the floor, indicated by the blankets and single pillow on the ground near the bed.

Oskai placed his bowl on the small table in front of the couch and began digging in. The others took up places around the room as they lowered their hoods, leaving me standing at the door.

"So, Oskai, what is your idea that you assume I will not like?"

That caught Edrah and Edsen's attention and they looked to our friend curiously.

Oskai finished with the bite he took and sat back in the couch with his hands clasped. "Before I start, let me catch them up on what we discussed earlier." Oskai turned to the siblings and told them of what I said about Sorden knowing we were there and how we needed to act now before it was too late. "Now that everyone is on the same page, and before I send out the messengers to warn the others in town, I think we should start a rebellion."

I frowned but it was Edrah who responded. "I thought that was what we were doing."

Oskai shook his head. "No, right now we are playing it safe. Hiding. Sneaking around. Trying to subtly change things. Now that Sorden knows we are here, it is only a matter of time before he starts a search party and hunts down anyone who looks like they would be against him. He knows we will try to rescue the royals so the palace will have too much attention on it. We need to draw the forces away from here."

"How do you suggest we do that?" Edsen asks, stepping closer and crossing his arms.

I sighed. "He has already said it. He wants to start a rebellion. A riot. In town. Am I right?"

Oskai pursed his lips and gave a single nod.

"Those are my people," I said. "Someone could get hurt."

Oskai held out his hand to me. "That is why I said you would not like it."

I started to pace, running the possible scenarios out in my mind. I wanted to avoid having a full out riot when we started this, but I should have known there would have to be some fighting. We had never gotten off that easily before. Why did my uncle have to make things so difficult? Could he not see what he was doing was wrong?

"We need to get the royals out," Edrah prompted.

I nodded and sighed. "I know. But is a full-scale rebellion necessary? Do we even have enough people to accomplish it?"

Oskai stood from his seat and stepped into my path, making me come to a stop.

"If we can get Cailyn's people and those from the mines it would be enough to cause a distraction. Messages have already been sent and they should be here soon."

I tapped my chin as I thought out his plan. "Cailyn's people are two days away. They should have received the message already and if they decided to come then they should be here any time now or at least a day out. We might not be able to count on them. The miners were close to Skorval already so maybe they are here and that would add some numbers." I sighed when I realized it could work and dropped my hands to my sides. "We will have to do this strategically. No random attacks and no citizens' lives caught in the crossfire."

"We need a way out, otherwise this rebellion plan will be for naught," Edsen said He uncrossed his arms and put his hands in his pockets. "The town will be too dangerous to take our parents and the others."

"I know a way to the docks from here if we can catch a ship," I said.

Oskai grinned. "It is a good thing Jasta and Gesebe came with a ship then."

I frowned at him. "But I thought they docked in Southern Shayd."

Oskai shook his head. "Technically, the Captain told her to meet us in Skorval so when they appeared at the mines instead, I asked Jasta about it and found out they had a ship at Skorval and made their way to us from there when they could not find us."

That was right! I had forgotten Kip asked them to meet us in Skorval. That meant we had a way out of there. We just needed to get to the docks with some brainwashed royals without being captured.

I stopped pacing and faced the others with hands on my hips. "Alright, we can have Gesebe, Shanm, and Cailyn start the riot. But we will need to time this just right. How about tonight, when the sun sets? That way it will give us darkness to hide and mobilize our people. But," I held up a finger, "No citizens or shops should be targeted. They do not deserve that, and it will only give the rebels a bad name."

"Agreed," the others said at once.

"I will send a message to the mines and to the town then," Oskai said as he walked to the door with his bowl. I was partly sure he wanted to go so he could also get another serving.

"Good, we will wait here."

Edrah and Edsen nodded, agreeing with my words.

When Oskai left, Edrah tackled me in another hug. I laughed as I stumbled back then set my friend away with two hands on her shoulders.

"Tell us what you have been up to," Edrah told me and grabbed my arms to guide me to the couch.

I frowned and started to shake my head, thinking we did not have time to catch up, but Edrah waved at me.

"It will be some time before the message is sent and we have to go to find their Majesties. Sit. Talk." Edrah plopped down on the seat in a very un-princess-like way and patted the spot next to her.

"She is right. We know where they are and it will be hours still until sunset," Edsen put in, siding with his sister.

I sat down and leaned into the cushions. "Fine. But you must tell me your story when I am finished."

Edrah and Edsen nodded then I went into my story from traversing the town with Gesebe to alerting Sorden of our presence in the mines. I felt as if I had repeated my story a hundred times by now, yet each time with a small new piece. When I finished, the siblings looked to one another grimly.

I held up my hands. "I know, I should not have attacked him. We would not be in a rush if I did not."

Edrah rubbed my back. "No, we understand. We would have done the same in your position."

Edsen snorted. "I would not have."

Edrah glared at him. "You are the most impulsive person I know."

Edsen grumbled but did not argue her point.

I shook my head with a small smile then turned to Edrah, dislodging her hand from my back. "Now tell me what you have been up to. Have you seen Their Majesties?"

"Yes, they are in their own wing of the palace. Guarded. But we posed as staff bringing them food to sneak in once."

"That head chef of yours made it possible. Thank the stars for that woman," Edsen added.

I nodded. "Dede is great. I am glad you were able to count her as an ally." I gestured to the cart of food. "It looks like we will use the same tactic."

"Yes, it is a good plan. Anyway, we saw our parents and the others. They each have their own room and it does not look like they talk to each other much. They looked like the living dead, Ana." Edrah's voice shook.

I shook my head. "He must have them dosed higher than anyone else to make sure they comply. I am assuming since you have Dede and the others in the kitchen free of skor, that they stopped serving dosed food and water to the royals. Have you seen any progress?"

Edsen came to the couch but since there was no room for him, he stood behind it. "Like she said, we have only seen them once. The head chef did not say anything about their countenance since then, but it has only been a day since they have ingested the skor. You know it takes at least three to get it completely out of a person's system. That is only if they do not also have a stone on their person."

I pinched the bridge of my nose. "This is going to be tough then."

"We never imagined it would be easy," Edrah said.

"What else have you been up to?" I asked.

Edrah looked to Edsen, the siblings communicating silently in the way Drislians often did, then she said, "We sent the team to search for skor and blend in to collect information on Sorden's plans. Edsen, Oskai, and I have been trying to get to the royals and stop access to skor through the kitchen. Sorden is gearing up for something big. It looks like what your friend told us about his plans may be true. He has been seeing a legal assistant lately and keeping the royals locked away."

The door opened, and Oskai came through. Our conversation petered off and we stared at him for news.

He waited until the door was closed and he was nearer before he explained, "The message is sent, the uprising will happen at sunset."

I look out of the window behind me. "That does not give us long."

"A few hours at least," Edsen added.

"So where is this back way out you spoke of?" Edrah asked me.

I nodded and pulled my attention away from the window. "Right. I used to climb down the mountain face a lot when I was young. There is an easy access to it from my rooms—"

"You cannot expect the royals to climb the mountain like some animal," Edsen interrupted.

I frowned at him and put my hands on my hips. Oskai walked over and thumped him on the back. Edsen spun toward Oskai, looking ready to start a fight.

"How dare you you—"

"Listen to her," Oskai interrupted.

I waited for both of them to look at me again before continuing. "First of all, you climbed a mountain just three days ago…like an 'animal'," I said with a roll of my eyes and air quotes, "and secondly, I was not going to suggest they climb down the mountain. It is too dangerous and if King Domen is anything like his son, he would not make it anyway. No, I was going to say, there is a thin, barely there, trail I made after Jasta escaped those years ago. I never use it, but I thought it would be a good emergency exit if the time came."

"'Thin? Barely there'?" Edsen asked and huffed in disbelief. "How is that any different?"

"Edsen, we can do it. It is the only way," Edrah said to her brother.

It *was* the only way. The royals could not rock climb down the mountain without Hooks and we only had two of those with us. We could not use a carriage or cart to take down the main path because there would be guards. We could not use the platforms because they would lead right into the middle of a riot and have guards posted there too.

"Let us take a look at this trail then," Edsen said, after his stare down with Edrah.

I nodded and led them out of the guest room then up the nearest set of stairs and down the halls to my rooms. I needed to change anyway. When everyone was inside, I gave them a moment to look around. I had known Edrah since we were young, but she had never been in my personal rooms. It was probably not as impressive as a room in a giant tree as they were in Drisl but mine were great in their own way. The sitting room we were in led into my bedchambers and a separate room off of that was my washroom.

While they took in everything, I walked to my closet and got out some black fighting pants, boots, and white shirt with my red jacket. After I was done changing into them, I braided my hair until I felt normal again.

"Ah, there is Anameta, fierce warrior of Skorval," Edrah said when I came out of the bedroom. The three of them were standing about the sitting room despite the couches in the middle.

I grinned at her, feeling more like myself and straightened my jacket. "Ready?" I asked.

I walked over to the doors that led to the balcony overlooking the sea and mountain below. It was how I got into the palace, and it would be how we got out. Glass was still scattered on the floor from when I broke in earlier and the sea breeze fluttered the white curtains.

The balcony was small, not enough for us all to stand together so one at a time I showed them the trail I was talking about.

"Where?" Edsen asked for the third time when it was his turn.

I stretched out a hand and pointed to the thin trail leading down the mountain to the left of the balcony. It was obvious to me because I created it but to the untrained eye, it was near impossible. Although, Edrah and Oskai did not have an issue spotting it.

"See there." I traced the path with my finger and Edsen's eyes followed.

I knew he finally saw it when his eyes widened, and he spluttered. "You have got to be joking."

Chapter 16

-Kip-

The man in the doorway, who I now recognized as the Overseer who escorted Sorden out, squeaked and darted away. At once, all of us sprang into motion and chased after him.

"Lenman, stay back and destroy the laboratory," I shouted behind me. I did not wait to see if he heard.

Jasta was ahead with Barent right behind her. I was surprised he was so fast, since he had trouble climbing the mountain to get there, but I guessed there was a difference between speed and endurance.

The Overseer started shouting for help. He turned back at one point long enough to throw his clipboard at Jasta who was gaining on him. She dodged it and leapt for him but missed by an inch. We were almost to the end of the hall which meant anyone from the circular room ahead would hear him.

Barent threw something ahead of him and hit the man in his legs, causing him to stumble. He righted himself quickly, but it was enough for Jasta to catch up and tackle him. When I reached them, I looked down to see what Barent threw. It was the satchel we brought with us that had my hat and jacket. I knelt down to it to check the bottles inside and sighed with relief when I saw none were broken. I lifted the bag and handed it back to Barent.

"Be careful with this. We cannot afford to lose any healing water. We may need it in the coming days."

"I think you meant to say 'thank you' and to that I say 'you are welcome,'" Barent said, panting next to me.

I glared and he took the bag sheepishly. "Right. Yes. Will do, Your Highness."

I shook my head and turned back to the Overseer who Jasta was hauling up from the ground.

Voices drifted to us from the end of the tunnel. The miners must have heard the man and were coming to investigate.

"Bring him," I said, and gestured to the other end of the tunnel, away from the voices.

Jasta took one side while Barent took his other and together they dragged him back the way we came.

The Overseer groaned then opened his mouth to shout but it was cut off when Jasta held a dagger to his throat. I had no idea where the dagger came from, especially since I knew Jasta preferred hand to hand combat, but I was not going to question it now.

"Where do we take him?" Barent asked.

As if emphasizing his question, the ground shook and rubble rained down on us from above. Sliding rocks from up ahead created a deafening sound in the tunnel. We all stopped and waited until everything settled before trying to move or talk. The Overseer whimpered, and a line of red dribbled down his neck from where the sharp metal pressed into his flesh.

Concerned shouts emanated from both ends of the tunnel we were in, and I knew we had limited time before they came to investigate.

"Good question," I said, remembering now that we could not go back to the laboratory.

Hurried footsteps pounded toward us, and I drew my sword, ready to fight if need be. A moment later, Lenman and Ren appeared, both grinning.

"All done," Lenman said. Then his smile slipped when he spotted the Overseer. "What do we do now?"

I looked both ways, wondering what the best route would be then an idea started to form.

I turned and started back down the path toward the circular mining room, away from the laboratory. "Come on, I have an idea."

I explained my plan as we walked, and we all got into position to play our parts. When I spotted the first miner of many huddling around the entrance to the tunnel, peering down it with curious and worried expressions, I started coughing and stumbling. Jasta, Barent, and Lenman followed and began their own distressed acts. The Overseer already looked injured and unwell without any acting, and he was…'convinced' not to speak as we came upon the miners.

"Oh my, are you alright?" one of the miners asked, taking in all of our appearances.

"What happened?" A guard demanded. It was then I noticed two armed guards eyeing the tunnel warily.

I pointed to the tunnel and faked a cough. "Explosion."

The miners gasped and looked to one another as they muttered their speculations and concerns. The guards looked to each other, concern and tension playing across their face as well.

The man who asked if we were alright placed a hand on his chest over his heart. "Is there anyone else?"

I shook my head. "Only us. We need some fresh air," I said and started for the tunnel that would lead us outside.

"Of course. We will need an official statement later though. If it really was an explosion then someone must have been trying to sabotage the work here." A guard said to us before shouting at the others to make room for us to pass. "Make way!"

The miners parted, leaving us a path between them.

"They are—" The Overseer started to say but yelped and snapped his mouth closed.

It seemed he needed a little more convincing and Jasta's obscured dagger at his back was doing the trick.

"Sir?" another miner asked, waiting for the man to finish.

The Overseer squeezed his lips together and shook his head.

I shook my head too and gave a fake sympathetic look to the man. "He needs some water. He got hurt in the blast." I pointed to his neck where the blood trail had dried and his dirty clothing from being tackled to the ground.

The miners nodded and ushered us to the tunnel on the opposite side of the room. A few handed us their canteens which we took a swig from for appearances. The Overseer did the same though his hands shook when he held it.

People watched us and whispered to each other as we made our way out of the mines. No one followed us once I assured them we could handle ourselves and that they should check on the damage to the tunnel instead. We knew the damage would only be to the laboratory and the storage room below, but it would get them off our backs for a while. I was sure they would start wondering about who we were and why we were in a secret room and why it exploded once they realized where the explosion occurred. By then, I expected to be gone from the area.

Outside, we took the trail leading to the first level of the mines then veered off to the side to go to the tents where we could have some privacy. We needed to know what the Overseer knew of Sorden and his activities in that laboratory.

Lenman led the way to their tents and I still wondered how he knew where his was when all the tents looked the same. We circled up in the same way we did earlier that day and sat the Overseer nearest the tent so he would be less likely to escape while the rest of us stood around him.

"Explain," I demanded.

The Overseer's eye widened and he shook his head. "I don't know what you're talking about."

Jasta raised her fist. At some point she put her dagger away without my notice. Now she resorted to her usual tactics of fighting.

The man drew back and held his hands up. "You cannot expect me to tell you my King's secrets. That is treason."

I straightened my back and glared at him. "I am your rightful King. I am Kipsien, son of King Karso."

The Overseer stared at me for a long time, his hands still raised in surrender. He almost reminded me of a statue with how still he sat.

Then he burst into laughter and looked around at all of us, wagging his finger in the air. "I have heard the rumors, but I did not believe them." He laughed for a moment longer than said through wheezing breaths, "You almost had me there."

Instead of saying anything, I took my signet ring on the string around my neck out of my shirt and held it out for him to see. I would have shown him my tattoo of the old compass crest on my arm but other than in Tripscari, tattoos could not prove anything.

The man's laughter died off as he took in the ring. He reached out with the same finger he had used to wave in the air and hovered over the metal. He glanced up at me for permission. I took it off and gestured for him to take it so he could inspect it closer.

"Impossible," he breathed.

"It is not impossible. He is right here. Living proof," Ren said. "And if you need anything further, I can vouch for him as can my father."

The Overseer arched a brow up at him. "Oh? And who is your father?"

Ren pushed his shoulders back, making his height tower over the man. "I am Prince Tlaren of the Islands of Tripscari."

The Overseer's eyebrows shot up. He looked at the rest of my group and gulped. He was probably assuming Jasta and Lenman were more than they seemed too. While they were Councilmembers of Under, that would probably not mean anything to him, so I stayed quiet and let him imagine.

The Overseer handed me my ring back and I put it around my neck and tucked it into my shirt. "Now. Talk."

He gulped again and looked at the others before focusing his attention on me. He wrung his hands and hesitated with his mouth open, trying to figure out what to say.

After a moment, he stilled his hands and frowned. "Why are you back now? Where were you all this time? King Sorden has been here for Shayd since your family…" his stern frown turned into a sympathetic one and his cheeks reddened. "Well, you know…" He waved a hand in the air as if dispersing the somber atmosphere he created. "Anyway, why should I tell you anything when my King has trusted me to keep his loyalty and secrets?"

"My answer to that is in the form of two questions. Do you know what he does in the laboratory? Do you know why the Royals are up in that palace?" I said, nodding toward the mines then pointing off into the distance toward the eastern mountain.

The Overseer scoffed. "Of course, I—" Then he frowned and looked down at his hands. "Well, maybe I don't. But what does it matter? He is the King, and I am only a commoner. He does not need to tell me anything."

Lenman put his hands on his hips and stared down at him. "Maybe you should learn to ask questions."

He looked up with wide eyes. "Of a King?" he spluttered for a moment then shook his head.

He looked as if he was about to have a conniption, so I eased the situation by taking back the lead in the conversation. "Let me tell you what he has been doing."

So, I explained what I had told about a hundred others at this point. How Sorden hired mercenaries to kill my family and all other heirs that tried to take over after. How he has manufactured mind manipulating skor and plans to take over the kingdoms with it. Then of what happened at the coronation and Shayd mines and finally our suspicions about why the royals were still in the palace.

The Overseer sat still for the whole tale and when I was finished, he looked at all of us anew.

"You can't be serious," he said.

"Would I lie about my family? Would he stand by my side if it were not true?" I pointed at Ren beside me.

The Overseer stood and placed his hands on his head. "This is insane. Things like this do not happen in the Four Kingdoms."

"Believe me, they do," I said somberly.

The Overseer sighed and his shoulders drooped. "Fine. I will tell you what I know."

He sat down again and proceeded to tell us what he learned in his time at the mines, which unfortunately for us was not a lot. He became Lord Sorden's trusted keeper of his secret laboratory years ago but never knew what happened inside. He was tasked to keep an eye on it from time to time and help sneak him in when the mines were busy. He told us that earlier that day Lord Sorden had been attacked in the tunnel and rushed off to alert his guards. I knew he was talking about Ana and Jasta, but I did not reveal it to him. He was told to tell the other Overseers about rebels and to keep an eye out for any suspicious behavior and to keep an eye on his laboratory because his key had been stolen.

After our talk with him, and confiscating his key, we sent him back into the mines to smooth over the chaos from the explosion and explain to the miners the truth of what happened.

"I think we should go to the palace. It sounds like trouble will be coming for those stationed there and they may need our help," I said to the others.

"You just want to see Ana," Ren said, nudging my arm and wagging his eyebrows suggestively.

I pushed him away from me and rolled my eyes, but I felt my cheeks warm and hoped they were not red for all to see.

Thankfully the others ignored him and moved our conversation back to the issue at hand.

"By now Ana should have gotten to the palace and met up with Oskai," Jasta said. "They will surely be planning something. I bet they are going to try to get the royals out today."

"Which means we should go now," I said and started to walk back toward the mines. I waited to speak until they were following me. "Someone may need to stay to lead the team here and respond to any emergencies though."

No one volunteered so I turned to them, forcing them to stop, when we got to the entrances to the mines.

"Barent cannot stay seeing as he is new. That leaves one of your three." I crossed my arms and waited.

Ren shook his head. "Well, I am going. My father is in there."

I nodded, agreeing with him and turned to Jasta and Lenman.

Before either could say anything someone shouted from behind us and ran over urgently. I did not recognize him and was ready to reach for my sword, but Lenman seemed to and stepped forward with a concerned frown.

"What is it? Are you coming from the town or the palace?"

Oh, so he must be one of the rebels. I wondered where they recruited him. Was he a miner from the Shayd Mines? Someone from the town below?

"I have a message from Oskai," he said.

Instantly we were all leaning forward to hear the message. Barent looked at each of us, confused but leaned in as well, sensing this name was important to us.

"Sorden knows there are rebels in Skorval. The palace team is going to try and get the royals out tonight. For a distraction, they want everyone to cause a riot. It will start at sunset."

The man let out a breath and put his hands behind his head, relaxing a little now that he relayed his message.

"Riot?" Jasta asked. "That sounds dangerous."

"Sunset?" Ren asked at the same time. "That is not too long now." We looked at the sky to mark the position of the sun. I would give it a couple more hours before things in Skorval got crazy.

The messenger straightened. "Oh, right. He said the riot should not hurt any citizens."

"Not hurt any citizens yet he wants a riot. What does he think is going to happen? Ana couldn't have agreed to this," Jasta said, shaking her head.

The messenger shrugged. "I am only telling you what Oskai sent me to relay here."

"Thank you, we will take it from here," Lenman told him.

The messenger nodded and headed back to the platforms that would take him down the mountain.

"What should we do now?" Barent asked.

I shook my head. "The plan stays the same, but now I will want two of you to stay here and the others to go to the palace. I trust Oskai, if he says there needs to be a riot tonight then there shall be one."

"This is crazy. We were going to go about this whole rebellion thing more subtly," Lenman said quietly.

I shrugged. "Well, sometimes, we need to do something big to be heard." I turned to Lenman and Jasta, all of us knowing already it would be those two who would stay behind. "Make sure your team knows not to hurt anyone, but cause some chaos, would you?"

Lenman sighed. "Ok, but be careful. You may not make it to the palace before the riots start."

"We will." I gave him a salute then gestured for Ren and Barent to follow me to the platforms.

"Thank the stars we are taking these this time," Barent said.

I chuckled but had to agree. All of this running around was putting some strain on my ribs and head. I had not been able to take any medicine recently and now I would have to run across Skorval. But it would be worth it in the end if we could end Sorden's reign tonight, once and for all.

Chapter 17

-Ana-

Once our plan was in place, a plan Edsen made clear he disapproved of, we decided to go retrieve the royals and get out of the palace. I opened my door to go back into the hall but a sharp point aimed at my chest kept me from going further. The others halted behind me wondering why I stopped. They could not see the threat from behind the half open door and I held a hand out behind me to keep them where they were.

I followed the sharp point up the weapon to the owner holding it and sighed when I saw the red coats of two of my elite warriors.

I held up my hands to show them I was unarmed and smiled. "Long time, no see."

Their frowns deepened and they continued to hold their defensive poses. With their red coats, extended blades, fierce frowns, and identical braided brown hair, they could be related. As it was, they were not related but everyone of the elite warriors regarded each other as family.

"What? No hello for your Saya?" I asked, trying to lighten the mood and get them to put their weapons down. They had not noticed the others in the room behind me and I was hoping to keep it that way for a little longer.

The one on the right, Nora, snorted. "A Saya does not betray her King and land."

The warrior next to her, Fayla, added. "Or her sisters."

I dropped my hands to my hips and nodded. "It would seem that way to you but how long have you known me? Would I do such a thing? Truly?"

They looked at each other and their frowns started to slip with their uncertainty.

"What has he told you?" I asked. I did not have to say any names, they knew to who I was referring.

They hesitated but eventually Nora answered. "He told us you have been brainwashed by pirates and now lead a rebellion. He has put everyone on alert. We thought if you were truly here then your rooms would be a good place to start looking."

With Nora's reminder, Fayla's frown turned fierce again and her sword arm straightened. "Yes, and he told us you attempted an assassination."

Nora stepped forward and pulled me out into the hall. "You may not be in your right mind, but we will fix that. You are under arrest."

"Wait, let me explain," I said, struggling against her. I did not want to hurt them, but I also could not let them take me to Sorden. I was readying myself for an attack when the door behind me opened further and the others stepped into the hall. Immediately, Fayla turned her sword on them and Nora positioned me so our backs were not to them which made us all form a circle.

"Princess," Fayla and Nora gasped.

Edrah's makeup had long since been washed away but she was still recognizable since she looked almost identical to her Queen mother. Edsen stood tall behind her, his eyes and hair indicating his relation to her. Oskai was the last one out and he eyed everyone warily, his fingers twitching toward his waistband where his sai were hidden.

"What is the meaning of this?" Nora asked.

"If you would have let me explain, you would know," I retorted.

"You were at the coronation and the Shayd mines, yes?" Edrah asked them.

Nora and Fayla shared a look then nodded.

Edrah continued. "You must have seen how strange both occasions were. The royals being taken away and hidden. Their children fighting alongside pirates and your Saya. Like she said, you know your Saya. She would do everything she could to protect her people. So, I ask you this, why would we side against Sorden?"

Nora's hold on me slackened and Fayla's sword arm drooped.

"We do not have time for this," Oskai growled in a low voice. That drew the two warrior's attention and they frowned at the bald man, full of suspicion.

Edsen stepped away. "He is right. We need to go."

Oskai popped back into the room and grabbed the cart of food then he and Edsen started to walk away, presumably toward the Kings and Queen. Fayla and Nora watched them, bewildered by their boldness.

I pulled away from Nora gently. "I have already talked to Shula." That name caught their attention and they gasped. "She has been investigating some things around here and knows I am of sound mind. I do not have time to explain right now but I ask you to trust me. We need to get the royals out of here."

Fayla and Nora looked to each other then at me and Edrah. As we waited for them to make a decision, precious time was being spent but I dared not rush them. They needed to be sure.

Finally, Fayla nodded and Nora gave her assent by sheathing her weapon.

"We will follow you and help you but one move we find suspicious and you are all being arrested," Fayla warned.

I nodded. They were only doing their jobs and I could not fault them for it.

"Then let us go."

We caught up to the men and together we all found our way to the royal hallway where Sorden's own rooms were along with the other royals. As expected, there were guards stationed at each end of the hallway but we took care of them quickly. We had the cart of food which got us passed them, then we quickly knocked them out from behind. I left Nora and Fayla to stand guard once the original guards were unconscious and hidden. They would be able to alert us if anyone came by and maybe convince them that they were assigned to guard the hall. It would be believable to almost anyone since the elite warriors were the fiercest fighters in Shayd and sent on dangerous or important missions all the time. Guarding royalty could be considered an important mission.

We stopped in front of the first door and Edrah breathed in deeply before opening it. "This is where my mother and father are."

She stepped through first, taking hesitant steps and the rest of us followed. Oskai stood near the partially open door to keep watch while the rest of us ventured further into the rooms. I did not know what I was expecting but the King and Queen of Drisl sitting in identical chairs facing one another and having tea was not it. They looked normal. The way Shula spoke, she made it seem as if the royals were mindless zombies.

Edrah approached them cautiously. They had not looked up from their tea when we entered and seemed oblivious still to our presence despite us coming closer into their line of vision. Only when Edrah was right next to her mother and the Queen still did not look up did I notice the subtle strangeness of their behavior. They seemed almost…mechanical.

Queen Emelda reached out and grabbed her cup, lifted it to her lips, then took a small sip and placed it down again only to repeat the whole process. King Darsen held his cup in his hand and looked down into it then up at his wife then at the table where the teapot and a plate of pastries sat then took a sip and repeated it all. I stepped closer and looked into their cups to see if they were empty but each cup held some tea. I did not think their tea was laced with skor knowing that Dede had been careful in giving the royals untainted drinks now that she knew of everything. Which meant they were still coming into contact with it some other way. It had been a couple days now so they should have been freed of it or nearly freed at least.

"Check them for skor then get them out of here, we will check the others," I told Edrah who stood close, peering at her parents worriedly.

"I am staying," Edsen said and went to his father to check him over.

I looked at Oskai but he only shrugged. It made sense he stayed there since there were two of them while the other rooms would only have one royal. So, we left the siblings to help their parents and went to find the others. Oskai took the room with King Domen, alone since Queen Rala decided to stay in Farlo with the young twins, while I took the one with King Trost.

King Trost used to be the only royal not influenced by Skor and helped us in our efforts to rid the Kingdoms of it. However, he was drugged at the coronation like the others and now sat in a chair facing the window gazing out at the sea. I looked for his staff, but it was nowhere to be seen. I approached him slowly.

"King Trost?" I asked.

He did not answer so I moved in front of him. He was different from King Darsen and Queen Emelda because he was not moving or imitating a normal action. He only sat in his chair and stared out of the window. I wondered if he chose to do that or if he was ordered to. Unlike the King and Queen of Drisl, King Trost was noticeably wearing skor. I took off the necklace and crown each embedded with skor then took a ring from each hand. I did not know why he had more than the others, but I suspected it was because he broke free of the skor influence once before. I tossed the items aside and helped King Trost stand. He obeyed but did not seem to know I was there.

By the stars, what was my uncle thinking treating the royals that way?

I led King Trost out of the room and met up with Oskai who escorted King Domen out of another room.

I glanced over King Domen looking for any injuries, oddities, and skor. He was taller than Oskai and leaned heavily on him though he did not seem to notice us or his surroundings just like the others. Oskai was able to keep him standing and maneuver him as he wished but I could tell it took a lot of strength.

I quirked a brow at Oskai conveying all my questions.

He nodded. "One piece of skor, a ring. He was just sitting on the edge of his bed staring at a wall. He was murmuring something, but I could not pick up what it was."

So, the only ones who had no skor on their person and were more animated were the Queen and King of Drisl yet they were just as lost in their mind as these two. I wondered why they were all so different.

"Let us go before someone notices they are gone."

We helped King Trost and King Domen down the hall. Just as we passed the first room, Edsen came out with his father's arm around his shoulders and Edrah came out behind him holding her mother's hand and dragging her along. We met up with Nora and Fayla down the hall and when they saw us, Nora helped Oskai with King Domen and Fayla helped Edsen with King Darsen. Together we moved along the white and gold palace halls keeping to the shadows and ducking around corners whenever a worker or guard came by. It was slow but we were almost there.

Just as we were about to head down the hall to my room, King Domen started muttering something.

"What is he saying?" I whispered back to Oskai.

We were walking in a line with me in front, Oskai behind me, and the others behind him in some order. It was useful for hiding our numbers and being able signal to the others when guards or staff were spotted.

There was a pause before Oskai whispered back, "I am not sure. It sounds like the same thing he was saying in his room, but I cannot make it out."

I listened hard as we walked, trying to make out his words. After a few moments, I whispered, "It is something about the sun and danger. Maybe he is remembering the beating sun in Farlo and how dangerous it is to travel in it?" It seemed random but he was a King who cared for his people, and he was not in his right mind currently.

"It is possible, but not really important right now," Oskai responded.

He had a point. I shut my mouth so we would be quieter as we traveled the last distance. I estimated we would arrive in a few minutes to my rooms and was too lost in my head thinking about the next part of the plan and King Domen's words so I did not realize the young woman standing in the hall, watering the various plants situated along the wall on pedestals until it was too late.

I stopped abruptly and the rest stumbled to a halt behind me. The woman's eyes looked up, having caught the motion of us in her peripheral vision, and stared at us wide eyed. Her hand halted in pouring water from her can and we stood frozen, waiting for her reaction. Oskai peered around me to assess the danger then sighed. He stepped around me and held up his hand in greeting.

His reaction was odd. I had never known Oskai to be friendly to a stranger before. He was the attack-now-ask-questions-later type. Yet, he approached the woman with a smile and calmly spoke to her. I was too stunned and wary to move so I did not hear what they said.

Edrah came up behind me and explained, "She is one of the rebels in our team. She was stationed here to keep an eye out on your rooms and the other warriors in this hall."

I looked back at my friend, my eyes widening at that information. Why was she not there the other times we had been around that hall? Unless she was and I never noticed. My eyes narrowed on the rebel girl as I tried to figure out if I recognized her.

"Now that you mention it, I have noticed her quite a bit over the last few days around here," Nora said. "I never suspected anything was off though." She snorted. "Wow, if I have learned anything from all this, it is that we have got to train better for this kind of stuff."

Fayla hummed her agreement.

Oskai returned and nodded to me, letting me know everything was okay and we could keep going. I looked at the girl one last time and she nodded to me before moving on down the hall and disappearing around the corner.

I shook my head both shaken and relieved by the experience. I waved my hand at everyone and we continued on the last little bit to my rooms.

The whole journey from the royals' rooms to here had been slow and we had a few close calls, but we made it. Now we had to somehow get them out onto a narrow path on the side of the mountain. I looked back at the royals and winced. Maybe this was not such a good idea. I led everyone into my rooms anyway, so we were not idling in the hall.

I dropped King Trost's arm and went to the balcony door, stepping through it and peering out at the trail again. I ran the scenario in my head then decided it was still the best option. There was no way we could just walk out the front doors with them. It was hard enough avoiding notice to get here.

"Okay, here is the plan," I said turning back to the group. "We are going to go one at a time and place the royals in between us so they have support from the front and back. They seem compliant enough, but I am worried about what they will do when faced with the great heights." I said the last bit with a pointed look at King Domen since I was having flashbacks of his son falling off the mountain.

"I will go first to lead the way," I pointed to King Trost, "Then him." I pointed to the others as I named the order we would be going out in, "Then Nora, King Domen, Fayla, Queen Emelda, Edrah, King Darsen, Edsen, and lastly Oskai." I quirked my brow at them all. "Does that sound good?"

They nodded.

"Good, now let us go."

I went out on the balcony and climbed carefully over the railing to the left that separated safety from the dangers of the cliff below. I planted my feet on the small trail then looked back and held my hands up to help King Trost. Nora helped him climb over the railing though he still had a blank look on his face. At least he was able to do this much.

I supported his weight until he had a good foothold on the ground then nodded to Nora behind him. Nora hopped over easily then turned back to help the next royal. I held my breath as King Domen climbed over, still muttering. I let out a breath once he was safely in line. It continued that way, the person in front helping those behind and as each new person got onto the path I moved forward more to make room. Finally, it was Edsen and Oskai left and I figured they had it in hand so I turned to start leading the way down, making sure to keep a hand on King Trost's forearm behind me.

A minute later, shouts had me looking over my shoulder, dreading the worst. Who had fallen?

But it was not what I thought.

The girl from the hallway, the rebel who was keeping an eye on my rooms and the other warriors, was leaning over the railing with her hands cupped around her mouth. I stopped, causing the others to halt too. I listened intently, wondering what she was shouting.

"They're coming!"

Just as her words reached me, guards started piling out onto the balcony followed by none other than my uncle. Sorden grabbed the girl by the arm and roughly shoved her back into my room then took her place on the balcony. My uncle glared at me, guards continuing to pile out behind him. The guards started shouting orders, both at us and each other.

How did they know we were out there?

No time to figure it out now.

I turned my back on the commotion and picked up my pace, leading King Trost by the arm behind me. I trusted the others to follow me. Despite the extra speed, we were still going too slow for my liking, but I had to be careful. The trail was too narrow, and one misstep could result in death.

Clanging metal made me turn my head to look behind me just in time to watch a guard plummet off the side of the mountain. I stared in shock at the disappearing guard then looked up to see if my group was okay. Oskai waved at me with a bloody sai to continue moving so I did. I continued to look back though as more clanging and shouts were heard and more bodies fell. Eventually there was only silence and I looked back to make sure everyone was still following.

It looked like the guards gave up and we were alone now. Oskai was breathing hard and kept one of his sai out just in case more guards came. The others looked worried but kept their focus on their next steps and on the person in front of them.

I let out a sigh of relief, the tension in my body loosening with the escaped breath. I still traveled quickly but did not look back again until we were nearly at the bottom of the mountain.

"Almost there," I told King Trost behind me, but I knew it was only for show. I was really reassuring myself.

I smiled when I stepped off the path to the ground at the bottom of the mountain and turned to watch the others make their way down too. When everyone was off the mountain trail and accounted for, I turned to the docks to search for the ship that would lead everyone to safety. We were on the outer edges and I knew most of the ships were docked further away. When I did not spot the pirates' ship right away, I assumed they did the same which meant we needed to get there without running into trouble.

Just as I had the last thought, a chorus of screams tore through the air. A moment later, a cacophony of shouts and clattering wood and metal sounded from the same direction. I did not realize Oskai stood next to me until he spoke.

"Must be the riots. It will be tricky getting the royals through it."

As soon as his words were spoken, new shouts came from the side of us. I looked sharply to my left and immediately grabbed my swords. Guards pointed at us and shouted to each other than at us. I did not know if these were guards from the palace, ones who did not fall off the mountain, and decided to cut us off down here or if they were already down here when the riots broke out and found us suspicious. Either way, we could not let them catch us.

"Run," I said.

We could have stayed and fought but I was hoping to get lost in the rioting crowd and slip away to the ship. Plus, the royals would hinder us, and I could not afford to lose now.

We all grabbed onto a King or Queen and dashed across the dockyard. It was not hard to find the riot. People ran in all directions while barrels and other smaller items were thrown into the air. People who I assumed to be rebels, clacked wooden sticks together at random citizens, causing them to scream and run away while others waved weapons threateningly at guards who were completely outnumbered by the rebels, yet they did not attack. I knew their orders were to defend but never attack, cause chaos but not so much that the citizens lost their livelihood. It was a fine line but one that could draw us support later or ruin us.

"There," Oskai said, pointing down a line of ships to one that had no distinct markings, name, or flags.

I knew it to be the pirates' ship and we directed our group to head for it. We were nearly there when a group of rebels jumped in front of us. I raised my swords but familiar red hair caught my attention. I lowered my weapons and grinned at the people in front of me.

"Cailyn, Shanm! Good to see you. Sorry I have not visited." I looked at the others in their group and spotted Cailyn's mother, sister, and father. They made it! Just in time.

Shanm ignored me, his focus on his father behind Oskai and me.

The other rebels in their group dispersed at Cailyn's signal and continued to cause controlled chaos on the docks, which kept the attention away from us for now. When her family did not move, Cailyn turned to them and whispered something. Sita, her sister, frowned but their mother grabbed the older girl's arm and dragged her away. Cailyn's father squeezed Cailyn's arm supportively then he glanced at us before leaving with the others.

Shanm approached his father and King Domen's eyes lit up as he reached for his son. His mutterings became louder and sudden realization dawned on me. I turned to Oskai and gripped his arm.

"Son. Danger. He was not talking about Farlo, he was talking about Shanm."

Oskai nodded and turned to the two Farloans with new understanding.

"Sorden must have had something awful planned for the crown prince," Oskai said.

"Well, we are almost to safety so let us load everyone up and get them out of here."

He nodded and together we rounded everyone up and ushered them onto the ship. I started to relax now that we were aboard, but someone suddenly burst onto the ship and I tensed again, expecting a fight. He was dressed in common clothes and held no weapon. I stared at the out of breath man suspiciously. His eyes glanced over me still looking for someone and when he spotted his target he advanced forward.

Immediately, Nora and Fayla blocked his way with swords pointed at his chest. His eyes widened and he held up his hands.

Oskai saw the commotion and came over. "It is ok, he is with us."

Nora and Fayla lowered their weapons and stood to the side but continued to look at him curiously. I went to stand by Oskai and gave him a questioning look.

"This is Gesebe's husband, Brenev."

I gasped and stared at Brenev anew. I had forgotten Gesebe was married. I wondered why he was not with her. I never noticed him in the first planning days before coming to Skorval either. Then again, I was too grief stricken to notice much of anything then. He was tall and must tower over his wife. His hair was a light brown and his brown eyes were shaped like most Shayds. I remembered Gesebe telling me back in Under that her husband was a miner once before.

I held out my hand. "Nice to meet you, Brenev. I am Ana."

He nodded and took my hand. "I know who you are. If you don't mind me saying, we don't have time for pleasantries. I saw a group of guards followed by Sorden coming this way."

I gasped and ran to the side of the ship. Sure enough, a squad of guards led by my uncle were storming through the riot toward us.

"We will hold them off," I said, gesturing to my warriors. "You two need to get this ship sailing, go to Under, or Tripscari, or Farlo. Give it a week then send someone to come back to check on us. If everything goes well, we should have won by then and I will be Queen." I told this to Oskai and Brenev.

Brenev nodded and went about doing what was necessary to sail and ordering the Princes and Princess around to help. Edrah gave me one last look before going off to follow his orders. Oskai continued to stand by me as I walked toward the gangplank. I stopped and turned to him, holding out a hand to stop him.

"I am coming with you," he said, his tone gruff.

"You cannot. Brenev needs help sailing and you are the only other one with knowledge of this ship."

Oskai glared at me then looked toward Brenev who was struggling with raising a sail then at the approaching guards. "There are too many of them, you will not be able to stop them. They may kill you and your warriors."

I looked to the approaching threat too and had to admit he was right. But I would not show my worry to him. "We will be fine. We have faced worse."

Oskai chuckled. "Like a group of pirates?"

I laughed. "Exactly."

Oskai growled after a moment. "Fine, but I will be back. Do not die."

I smiled and gave the gruff man a hug. He patted me on the back then pushed me toward the exit.

I started to walk off the ship when a woman with red hair flew to my side. "I'm coming too."

I glanced at Nora and Fayla but they shrugged, leaving it up to me.

I turned to look at Cailyn again. "Good to have you. Now let us go stop Sorden."

Chapter 18

-Kip-

Lenman's words were truer than I would have liked. We had just stepped off the platform at the bottom of the mountain when we heard the shouts. We were in one of the outer rings so we still had a while to go before we reached the town, yet we could hear the chaos beginning. I looked at the sky which had not quite reached sunset yet.

I shared a nervous look with Ren. The rebels had begun early.

"Do you think we will make it?" Barent whispered despite us being the only ones around.

I squashed the nerves and put on a brave face and slapped Barent reassuringly on the back. "Sure we will. Now we should go before it gets dark."

I put my dark blue coat and tri-pointed hat on, feeling more like myself before leading them through the rings of Skorval and into town. The rebels from the other rings must have congregated in the center ring of Skorval because there were much more people running about throwing things and waving weapons threateningly in the air than I would have expected. On closer inspection the weapons were broken pits of wood or rocks. I watched some run by shouting nonsensical things at the citizens who cowered in doorways or ran about screaming. None of the rebels were striking any of the citizens so it was only to scare them. A moment later a group of guards burst into the area and started attacking the rebels who then fought back in defense and scattered only to reappear somewhere else.

We did our best to skirt around the mayhem and slowly made our way toward the path that would lead to the eastern mountain where the palace was held.

Barent ducked and brought me down with him just as a rock flew over our heads. I spun around, ready to scold the rebel who had done it but noticed the guards were tossing the weapons of the rebel they had captured without any care who might be in the way. They probably figured they would blame any injuries on the rebels. I shook my head in disgust and straightened, continuing on my way but more vigilant of the people around me.

I was just thinking it was nice that no one was paying us any attention since they were more focused on the chaos in their town when someone grabbed my arm and brought me to a stop. Noticing my abrupt stop, Barent spun around with wide eyes, thinking we had been attacked and Ren held up his fists ready to free me but stopped when he saw who it was. I followed his gaze to the short woman with shoulder length brown hair staring at me with wide eyes. Another woman in a red coat stood next to her looking at us with interest but she kept glancing at our surroundings and had her hand placed on her sword at her side as well. I tensed, expecting the warrior to attack us but she seemed to be protecting us instead.

"Captain! What are you doing here? I thought you were going to the mines." Gesebe said, bringing my attention back down to her.

"I need to get to the palace. We are going to help Ana and the others. They are in danger."

Gesebe slapped me on my arm. "It is dangerous for you to be out here. We cannot have you dying a second time."

Barent gasped, then stifled a laugh. He was not used to so many people being familiar enough with a Prince to get away with slapping him.

I scoffed and moved my arm out of range of her attack. "I will be fine as long as my own people stop slapping me."

Gesebe ignored my comment and changed the subject, her features softening as she spoke. "Have you seen Ana yet?"

While I would have liked that, I had not run into her yet. I had missed her by a few minutes at the mines. My hope was we would make it in time to see her at the palace. My heart picked up its pace at the thought of seeing her again.

Someone slammed into me, knocking me against the nearest building. My friends shouted my name, but none could get to me as chaos suddenly erupted.

The body that had hit me was an unconscious man. I looked up to see where he had come from and saw guards attacking my friends. Not just them but anyone in sight. I knew for a fact the people huddling against walls and doorways were not rebels, but the guards were attacking them anyway. I shoved the unconscious man from me and jumped in just in time to stop a guard from smashing the hilt of his sword on a young woman's head. I caught the guard's wrist and yanked so his aim was off and hit the wall next to her instead. She screamed and ran away while the guard turned to me with a fierce glare. I pulled my sword.

"You have no right to be attacking innocents."

He sneered. "Innocents? These people are traitors to the crown and will go down with the other rebels."

"They were not doing anything!"

The guard smirked. "Sorden will not know that."

The guard attacked. He was too clumsy and relied on brute strength which was easy to maneuver passed. It was not too hard to get around his blade and stab him. I looked around for my friends and saw Barent and Ren battling a couple of guards. Barent was mostly running away and chucking things back at them. Ren was wrestling his opponent across the ground. Gesebe had the woman elite warrior with her and together they fought a couple guards who were harassing some townspeople.

I saw a guard point his blade at Gesebe's back, my friend oblivious to the incoming attack, so I launched myself at him and parried his blade before it hit. Two strikes and he was out.

I went around helping each of my friends until the guards had either run off to another part of the town or were lying dead on the ground.

I stood with my sword in the middle of the road, breathing heavily, tensed for another attack. Gesebe put her hand on my arm and I relaxed when I saw no one else was going to attack us.

I shook my head then looked toward the eastern mountain. "We really need to go."

Gesebe nodded and gave me a serious look. "Right, they are probably already attempting to get the royals out. Here, take Shula with you."

At her name, the warrior by her side focused on us again and nodded her head. "Good idea, I am sure you can handle this," she said to Gesebe. "I am worried about the others up there."

Gesebe smiled and nodded at her new friend then shooed her away.

I smiled a little too. It was not every day I saw someone trust in Gesebe's abilities and not underestimate her.

"Let us go then," I said.

"Come, I will show you a quicker way," Shula said and took the lead.

The sun was dipping lower and lower as we traversed the inner ring of Skorval and a path that cut through the other rings, directly to the palace mountain. There were more guards running around than I thought existed in Skorval, but I had to remember Sorden got other units from some of the other royals when he controlled them before.

The only guards who were not running about trying to tame the chaos were the three at the platforms leading up the mountain. They had their weapons out and studied their surroundings with a vigilance that would be hard to sneak around.

Shula stopped us from going further when we reached a building, a guard house or something, and had us hide behind it while she took care of the guards. The three of us peeked around the wooden building to watch Shula dispose of the guards.

She talked to them for a minute, words we could not hear from our position, but whatever they said caused a small frown to mar her friendly demeanor. She waved to the guards then got onto the platform as if she was about to go up the mountain. I tensed, expecting her to go without us and I immediately started making a plan for how to get up the mountain now. We had Hooks, well Ren and I did, so we could climb.

Before I had a full backup plan formulated, Shula struck the guards from behind and a small battle ensued which she finished quickly. They had no reason to turn and watch her ascent since she was supposed to be loyal to Sorden as an elite warrior, so she had the element of surprise on her side. When all three guards laid on the ground unconscious, I rushed out from behind the building.

Shula beamed at me with her hands on her hips. "Why do you look so worried, Prince? Afraid I would go on without you?"

I shook my head. "Of course not." Then I got onto the platform beside her, Ren and Barent following close behind. She did not need to know I had doubted her.

"What did the guards tell you? You looked like it was bad news," Ren said as we started our ascent.

Barent gripped the rope nearest him and looked down as we continued to rise. I was about to make a quip that he could go up the path instead of platform if he was nervous of the height, but I wanted to hear Shula's answer and instead turned to her waiting for her to speak.

Shula's frown reappeared and she crossed her arms. "The royals got out and have escaped on a ship with some of the rebels and Princes and Princess."

Ren and I shared a relieved smile. However, a part of me was a little sad I had missed her again.

"That is great!" Ren exclaimed. But our smiles slowly faded as we realized Shula was still frowning. "But why are you not happy?"

Shula looked up toward the top of the mountain. "Ana has been captured. She and two of my sisters have just passed this way not too long ago in custody. Honestly, I am surprised the guards let me pass seeing as how I am an elite too, but their mistake is our gain."

"Sorden has Ana?" I asked even though I heard her clearly.

"This is bad," Ren said and looked to me with concern.

"Don't worry, we will get her," Barent said trying to reassure us, but he was new, he did not know what Sorden was capable of. Thankfully, none of them knew I was alive, and we could use that to our advantage.

At the top, Shula guided us to the side of the palace instead of going up to the main doors. Even from the platforms we could see the main entrance was guarded and I did not think we would have the same luck we had below. The side entrance was more of a gate that led into a courtyard. I spotted weapons on racks nearby and fighting dummies near the edges. It must have been where the guards and elites trained. However, no one was there at the moment and we slipped past the courtyard to the door that led inside.

Before pushing it open, Shula hesitated and turned to us. "I think they are being held in the dungeons. They have not been in use as long as I have been here but that seems a likely place to hold rebels. We should check there first. It will be near impossible to get in though since it is in a deeper part of the mountain, and it will surely be guarded."

I looked to Barent and Ren who nodded back at me. I turned to Shula to give the order. "Lead us there. We will get them out."

She looked me up and down from head to toe, a hint of disbelief in her eyes, but she nodded anyway and opened the door to lead us to the dungeons. She spoke quietly to us along the way.

"Ana made sure each of us knew the route to the dungeons in case we ever needed to hold someone there. However, there was never a need, the people of Skorval have always been peaceful. I guess I know partly why now. Sorden would surely not allow his own people to act out in any way that would make him look bad."

She held up her hand signaling to us to stop. Then she peered around the corner. When she checked it was all clear she dropped her hand and turned left down the next hall which I could see now led to a set of stairs. Shula drew her weapon before descending them.

"Prepare yourselves. I do not know who is down here. It could be one or even twenty guards. It could be my own sisters."

I drew my sword but Ren and Barent did not have one, so they clenched their fists preparing to fight hand to hand if need be.

The stairs continued, spiraling down, for what seemed like forever. The farther we went, the darker and colder it became. Barent audibly shivered behind me, the only sound other than our feet on the stone.

I knew we were at the end when Shula slowed. We stopped behind her and listened.

Voices could be heard not too far away, two from the sound of it. That either meant there were only two guards or the two speaking had a silent audience in which there could be many more just around the bend.

Shula took a chance and peeked around the wall then suddenly burst into action, leaping the rest of the way down and around the bend. I heard surprised shouts and two thuds before there was silence again. It all happened faster than any of us could react.

I ran the last few steps and saw two guards unconscious on the ground. Ren whistled behind me, impressed by her speed and strength. Shula searched them for keys then unlocked the gate that separated the stairwell from the dungeon.

We moved quietly still, even though our presence would have been heard by now and alerted any others. No one else met us as we traveled past the various cells until we found one that was occupied.

Shula sheathed her sword then gripped the bars. "Nora, Fayla!"

Three women inside quickly stood and rushed to the bars.

"Shula, what are you doing here?" One of them asked.

Two of them had red coats and their hair braided so it was hard to distinguish them. It was dark, with the only light being from the lantern back down the hall near the entrance, so if they had any identifying marks, I could not see them. However, the third woman I knew right away.

"Cailyn!"

Their attention caught on us and the two warriors eyed us curiously. Cailyn however stared at me with wide eyes.

"Your Highness? But…how?"

"I will explain later."

"I heard about the capture and figured this was a likely place to hold rebels for now," Shula explained as she unlocked their cell. "I thought it was a good place to start anyway. But where is Saya Ana?"

She swung the door open and the women rushed out. Cailyn came to stand in front of me, continuing to stare in awe and confusion.

The warrior on the right responded, oblivious to my encounter with Cailyn. "Sorden took her with him while we were escorted here."

The warrior next to her added, "I heard something about the throne room."

Shula shook her head with worry. "We have to find her."

Nora and Fayla nodded and the three of them started back down the hall. We followed after them and I put my sword away now that the danger seemed to be gone.

"What happened?" I asked Cailyn, as we followed the warriors out of the dungeon. Ahead of us Nora and Fayla were speaking with Shula, each of them explaining their journey up to now.

Cailyn shook her head. "We were holding off a bunch of guards so the ship with the royals could sail away and got overwhelmed."

"I am glad they only captured you and did not kill you all on the spot."

"What about you?" She asked, unable to let me avoid how I survived. "What happened to you after the fall?"

I patted my side where the Hook rested and smiled to myself. "I finally remembered to use the Hook."

Ren patted me on the shoulder, having been listening to our conversation. I spared him a smile before continuing with where I woke up and made my way there, finding Barent along the way and how we came to be at the palace. Only after I was finished did I notice the three warriors in front of us were quiet and listening to me as well.

"Ana will be happy to see you," Cailyn said after a moment of silence.

"I am looking forward to it."

We climbed back up the spiral staircase then walked together down the hall, no longer trying to hide our presence. People stared at us curiously and some with wide knowing eyes. Others only glanced at us as they ran about, terrified by the riots going on everywhere in Skorval. I paid them all little attention. My whole focus was on seeing Ana again and hoping her uncle was not torturing her.

Guards were stationed in front of the large doors that I assumed led to the throne room since that was where we were headed. The guards spotted us and for once did not hesitate at the red coats the warriors wore and attacked immediately. We barely had to stop as the warriors quickly dispatched them and Nora and Fayla threw the doors open.

I drew my sword and stormed in, the others right behind me with their fists or weapons out too. I scanned the room and spotted Ana immediately. I grinned and opened my mouth to call to her, but something was off.

I stopped in my tracks to take everything in, trying to process what I was seeing.

Her green gaze locked on me, but her eyes were cold and unfamiliar. She pulled her swords from behind her back and crouched in a guarded stance.

"Ana?"

"Drop your weapons and surrender," she said in return.

Chapter 19

-Ana-

My warriors stood around the Captain looking from me to him with confusion. Well, some of my warriors. There were technically five of them, and two of them stood behind me, loyally awaiting my orders and guarding my back. Unlike those traitors across the room.

"I said, drop your weapons," I repeated and took a step forward. Moira and Lani behind me stepped forward too, Moira swinging a set of nunchucks around while Lani angled her spear point toward the threat.

The guards stationed in a semi-circle behind me and my warriors stayed where they were but I heard the sliding metal of their swords as they pulled them free of their sheaths.

"Ana?" The Captain repeated, looking more hurt by the second.

I did not know why he was pretending to care about me when all this time he had been manipulating me and holding me prisoner. Turning me against my own kingdom. My own family. I sneered at him with disgust. How had I ever trusted him?

A small part of me longed to reach for him. He was alive. He was actually, really alive. That should have been a joyous occasion.

I stamped that part down, disgusted that his manipulation still had a hold on me. I did not care how he survived. He probably faked the death to manipulate me and all the others even more. Thankfully, my uncle got through to me and showed me the truth.

Just as I had the thought, King Sorden chuckled behind me and came off the dais to stand by my side. Moira made room for him, careful not to hit him with her nunchucks as she continued twirling them around.

"Captain! What a surprise. How *did* you survive that fall?" Sorden waved his hand in the air. "Ah, never mind. You are here now. Just in time, in fact. We can start with you.”

“What did you do to her?” He nearly growled and him and his group moved forward until they were only ten feet away.

I tensed, eyeing them all and waiting for one of them to move in for the attack. They would not get far before I rammed my sword through their chest. I hoped my fierce gaze expressed it so.

“Captain, look around her neck,” Cailyn said.

The Captain’s gaze, along with everyone else in his group, zeroed in on my chest where my necklace with a large skor stone laid. I did not know what was so fascinating about it, but it had them frowning and looking to one another with concern.

Maybe they hoped to steal it from me, but the thought was laughable because they would never get close enough to do it.

“Ana, this is the man who tried to kill me, steal you away, and ruin Shayd after all of our hard work. Kill him,” My uncle said, calmly.

I narrowed my eyes and zeroed in on my target. The others in the Captain’s group tensed and lined up in front of him which he seemed not to like because he tried pushing his way through the barrier, but they did not budge. I looked to Moira and Lani and tilted my head toward the traitors. They nodded and shouted for the guards to join them before leaping forward to attack and divide the defending group. I waited a moment for the elites warriors and guards to split the traitors up before I leapt toward the center, my swords aimed at the Captain, but a body moved in the way before I made it and Shula blocked with her long, single sword.

"Shula," I ground out as I fought against her strength. "Why are you doing this?"

"Saya, you are being controlled by Sorden. This is not you."

I laughed and shoved her away before attacking her one sword at a time which made her work twice as hard to deflect both of them.

"Ana," The Captain called to me from behind Shula, "you know me. I know you. Snap out of it."

I threw a glare his way and tried to dart around Shula to stab him but she blocked my way once again. Another body came into the fray, standing by Shula's side and towering over me.

"Ana, if you do not listen to them then at least listen to me. Sorden is controlling you with that skor around your neck. You are on our side."

I swiped at Ren halfheartedly, seeing as he was unarmed and my best friend, but he easily dodged it.

Why was he siding with the enemies? He should not be there. I knocked Shula's sword out of her hands with one blade and cut her arm with my other. She hissed and stepped backward, her hand covering the injury. The Captain did not hesitate to take her place and this time he raised his sword in defense.

A guard came at him from the side but even though Kip looked like he was distracted by his focus on me, he easily spun to avoid the blade and stabbed the guard in the back. The guard shouted in pain and fell to the floor, his momentum making him slide a couple feet.

I dropped into a guarded stance and raised an eyebrow tauntingly.

"I guess we will finally get our duel after all," I said, smirking.

"I do not want to fight you." He said, his eyes pleading with me.

"Ana—" Ren tried once again but a guard lunged at him before he could say more and took his focus from us.

I ignored him and swiped at the Captain. He easily dodged and I lunged for his open side which he twisted away from. He winced slightly but it was enough to show me a weakness I could exploit. It looked like he was not totally unharmed from his fall after all.

We circled each other, searching for an opening. Suddenly he stopped and lowered his sword. Shocked by his action, I did not immediately attack.

"I bet you cannot fight me without that stone around your neck?" He taunted.

I frowned. "What?"

He made no sense. What would my skor stone have to do with my fighting ability?

I shook my head and swung both my blades, aiming for his head. His brows shot up and he stepped back and blocked with his sword. He pushed me back then kept his blade up this time to defend himself but did not initiate an attack. Instead, he tried to taunt me again.

"Are you afraid you could not beat me without your uncle whispering orders in your ear?"

Technically, Sorden was still near the dais, watching the fights around the room with a small smile, oblivious to our conversation and certainly not whispering anything to me.

I stabbed at him repeatedly as I spoke, "What are you talking about?"

He countered every move.

"Take it off and you will see."

My uncle gave me the necklace earlier tonight as a coming home present. He had been worried about me since I had been kidnapped and attacked him at his coronation and again at the mines. He was worried I had been brainwashed by the pirates beyond repair, but thankfully, once he took me back to the palace and talked to me, I finally felt I knew what was right. The past few days seemed to be a blur and I could barely remember my actions, but I knew I acted against Skorval and that was no way for a Saya to behave. I did not want to take the necklace off. It was special to me. A token from my uncle.

I shook my head and lunged at the Captain.

"She is not going to take it off," Ren said through heavy breaths to the Captain. I guessed he defeated his opponent then. "You will have to take it."

The Captain looked frustrated but nodded at Ren behind me before launching into a series of attacks that had me backing away and defend for my life. He had been holding back more than I thought.

Back and forth we struck, ducked, rolled, and circled. Sweat beaded on my chest and forehead. My arms were beginning to feel strained, but I knew he was tiring more quickly than me. His steps faltered more than naught, and his strikes seemed weaker.

I smiled, predicting I would have him beat in four moves. I stepped forward and used one of my swords to slash at his right arm, but he easily deflected it with his sword. I used my other sword immediately on his left, near his head. He had to duck so I used the distraction to step into his space and punch his left side with the pommel of my right sword. He cried out and doubled over, clutching his ribs with one hand and loosely holding his sword with his other. My final move was to disarm him and knock him down, so I was towering over him and he was splayed on the floor.

I smirked down at him and pulled an arm back to stab him. He stared up at me with wide, fear filled eyes. Something else flashed in them but I did not get a chance to decipher it. Someone pulled at my necklace from behind, choking me until I turned to see who it was and relieve the pressure on my neck.

Ren had the chain gripped in his hand, looking down at it, shocked that it had not come off when he yanked on it. I growled and swung at him. He did not back away like I thought he would and instead yanked harder on the chain. It jerked my head down with the force, throwing my aim off. I missed him by an inch.

Finally with one more tug, the chain broke and my skor necklace fell to the ground. I gasped and reached for it, but Ren kicked it away before I could touch it. I looked up, mouth agape at my friend. He had never done something like that before. What was his deal?

My neck ached from where the chain had dug into my skin, but it was the least of my problems right now. I straightened and faced off against Ren who was unarmed.

He held his hands up and shook his head. "Do not attack. I am trying to help you."

I started to lunge at him when a strong set of arms banded around me from behind.

I shrieked and struggled against the hold. Ren stepped forward and yanked my swords away so I was the one unarmed.

The Captain's voice spoke from behind me, informing me whose arms were holding me. "Ana, snap out of it. We are not going to hurt you."

I snorted. "Could have fooled me. I am guessing this hold is just a hug then? Or that Ren having my swords is not a threat?"

The Captain chuckled and whispered into my ear, sending tingles along my skin. "It could be a hug if you would let me."

His hold slackened and I was suddenly pressed against his body in a whole new way. His head rested on my shoulder and his breaths tickled my ear. My body froze, unsure what to do about the strange and unexpected turn of events. I was sure I should head butt him and kick him in the shin but that hold felt…comfortable, safe, and warm. I did not want to leave the embrace but that made no sense. He was my enemy.

Just as I started to remember he was my enemy and I should pull away he whispered again in my ear, only for the two of us to hear.

"I missed you. I never thought I would see you again. Ana—"

His voice cracked sending a spear into my heart. It felt like a wall of ice I had around it was thawing, and my walls were crumbling. I was so confused about how to feel. Part of me wanted to fight him, another part wanted to kiss him.

"Ana, I love you." Then he pressed his lips so softly it could have been my imagination on my neck just below my ear.

And that was it.

Whatever spell had been over me dissolved and everything came rushing back. My uncle's skor manipulation. The royals. Our adventures together up to now and his fall.

By the stars and sea, Kip was alive!

I spun around in his arms. He tensed and looked at me warily, expecting me to attack. But I was smiling, tears pooled in my eyes.

"Kip," I breathed out then kissed him.

His arms relaxed more, and I was able to pull my arms free and ran my fingers up his neck and into his hair, knocking his hat off. The brief kiss in the tent at the mines was nothing compared to this one. I poured everything I felt into the kiss. My grief. My relief. My joy. My heart exploded at his touch, and I felt like I was going to dissolve into a puddle.

After a few moments, Kip pulled back and chuckled, bringing up one of his hands to my face and rubbing away the tears I did not realize were falling.

He leaned down and kissed me one more time then said the three little words that would forever be magic to me. "I love you."

I grinned. "I love you too."

I did not know how I was able to break away from the skor spell so easily. Maybe because I did not have it on for long? Whatever the reason, I was extremely grateful for it and so relieved I had not killed him.

He pulled me tighter against him and we just stayed like that for a few more moments until Ren cleared his throat, drawing our attention to him.

He was smiling but his eyes looked worried as they flitted about the room. "This is lovely, truly, but might I remind you we have a bit of a situation going on right now?"

Kip and I pulled apart and looked around the room. Lani, Moira, and a few guards were still battling the others. Shula was off to the side watching them and clutching her wound.

Ren handed me my swords again, and I gratefully took them, settling my palms around the hilts and rubbing the glass stones embedded in them.

I looked for Sorden near the dais but was shocked to find him missing.

No, no, no. He could not escape again.

I spun in a circle and just as I laid eyes on him, he let out a battle cry, rising from behind Kip with a dagger aimed at his back.

Kip started to turn but it would be too late. Ren cried out and reached for him, but a guard inserted himself in his path and Ren had no choice but to fight him or die. I was the only one in position to do anything.

I dropped my left sword and pushed Kip out of the way with my now empty hand. Now Sorden's momentum was taking him to me. His eyes widened but he could not pull back in time. I raised my right sword and struck up into his chest. His body halted and his wide eyes looked down at the blade protruding from him. I yanked it out and stepped back only then noticing the same thing happening to me. As I stepped back, my uncle's dagger slipped free of my body, the area just above my heart, and I gasped. The pain hit me like a tsunami and I fell to my knees. My sword clattered to the ground and I fought the urge to pass out.

Sorden gasped and held his wound with both hands, but blood gushed too much for his pressure to do anything helpful. He looked down at me, anger and fear in his eyes.

"I was only doing…what was best…for Shayd," He gasped out.

I shook my head, gritting my teeth through my own pain and managed to say steadily, "No, uncle. You were being greedy and selfish and manipulative. I am sorry it ended like this, but you left me no choice."

He reached out a bloody hand to me and took a step forward. "Ana—" Then he frowned and raised his blade, aiming for me. "I am sorry too." Then the blade plunged down.

I closed my eyes, waiting for it to be over but nothing happened. A moment later I cracked open my eyes to peek out at my uncle and saw his wide eyes blank and unseeing in front of me. He had another blade through him, the handle of it intricate and fancy. It was Kip's.

Kip yanked it out and stood over his body as Sorden collapsed. I opened my eyes all the way to look down at him. Next to his body was a severed hand and a bloody dagger. Kip must have chopped off his hand before he could stab me again.

I promised myself I would kill Sorden and now that I had, *we* had, I did not feel any better. Watching him die would forever be imprinted on my mind. But for what he had done to Kip's family and all the other successors, to the royals, to those who died on the merchant ship, and all those he manipulated with skor, he deserved it.

Kip and Ren, who must have defeated the guard, dropped down next to me. Kip laid me back and cradled my head in his lap. He brushed my hair away from my face with one hand and held a small vial with the other.

"This might sting a little," he said calmly as Ren peeled my jacket away from the wound.

I hissed and tried to roll away, but Ren held me down.

Slowly, Kip poured the healing water over the wound, needing the whole vial it seemed. Ren and Kip waited with bated breath for it to do its work. The pain was still so intense the edges of my vision started to go black.

I breathed harder trying to get oxygen into my lungs, but it was difficult. Then, finally, the pain started to fade and I could feel my skin stitch together. It felt like minutes before it was done and I could breathe better.

Ren checked over the area and nodded his head. "You will probably need a lot of rest, but it is healed."

Kip sighed in relief and lifted me so he could hug me tight. I clung to him, aware my blood was covering us both but not caring. Right now, I just needed Kip.

"What did you do?!"

Our heads spun toward the voice and saw Moira staring at us, wide eyed then down at her King. The fighting around the room had stopped. Many of the guards' bodies laid around the room unmoving but many still were alive and stared at us with shock.

I stood, slowly and with Kip's support, then stepped away from the Prince and approached my friend. My sister. My warrior.

"It is a long story. But trust me. It was necessary. I mean, he did just try to kill me after all but that is only the start of his problems."

Shula came up to us, her arm now bandaged in a ripped piece of clothing. Kip immediately went to her and gave her some healing water too. She stared down in wonder as the wound vanished.

When it was done she turned to Moira. "I can explain. Well as much as I know anyway. I am sure we will all need a full account soon."

"Yes, once we clear everything up, a full account will be told." Louder, so everyone in the room could hear I announced, "For now, we have a new King to appoint."

We must have been a sight to see. Appointing a new King while half of us were covered in blood and the old King lay only feet away. We faced Kip who straightened and took a ring on a cord from around his neck. He tossed the cord aside and placed the ring on his finger.

"I, Kipsien, son of King Karso, claim the throne of Shayd and become its King after the fall of the false ruler and traitor Sorden."

All of the warriors and guards gasped at the declaration. I smiled and winked at him which made him relax. I knew he was probably freaking out inside and wanted him to know I would have his back. Always.

"All hail, King Kipsien!" I shouted then took to one knee and bowed.

Ren immediately copied my declaration and bowed, though as a Prince, he only had to incline his head. The others in the room, except the very confused guards, fell to the floor and bowed as I did. Kip glared at the remaining guards but one of them stepped forward, brandishing his weapon.

"You are not our King! You are a traitor and assassin!"

The man ran froward, aiming for Kip. However, there were too many people between the guard and Kip for it to be a concern. Fayla stood then held out a blade just in time for the guard's momentum to carry him onto it. The man collapsed and the other guards immediately fell to the floor in a bow.

"Rise, loyal warriors," Kip said formally.

We all stood and I went to Kip, throwing myself into his arms.

He may have been King now, but that would not stop me from showing him how much he meant to me.

I kissed him as he lifted me off my feet and everything, for the first time, felt right.

When we had to pull back for air, we could not stop grinning.

He placed me on my feet but held onto my hand. Kip stared into my eyes, so much passing between us in the span of a moment.

Suddenly he tugged me closer to him and softly said, "Marry me, Anameta, Saya of the elite warriors and bearer of my heart."

I gasped and searched his eyes to see if he was serious. What I saw reflected in the brown depths sent warmth throughout my whole body and with it a sense of love and purpose settled over me.

"Yes, of course." Then I kissed the King of Shayd/Captain of pirates.

Epilogue

-Ana-

I said yes, of course, but stipulated I would marry him later only after everything was settled.

It took weeks.

The word was sent out about Sorden's betrayal and death. Skor was recalled across all the kingdoms and destroyed. Jasta eventually read through the alchemy book they discovered in the secret laboratory and found out the skor only had manipulative properties when bathed in a certain serum mixed with blood. Even though Sorden was dead and the skor was tied to his blood and therefore unable to control anyone now, we still destroyed it to be safe.

Kip had shut down the skor mines until we could get all the altered stones out and the mines cleared. It would be some time before people wanted to buy skor anyway since the story of what Sorden did with the stones had spread. Instead, Kip opened the Shayd mines and outfitted the miners with new technology and equipment. Cailyn's father was put in charge of the mines, and everyone seemed much happier with the new arrangements.

Cailyn's village was seen to despite their insistence they did not need anything. Women were reunited with their loved ones from the mines and the village road was widened with their permission. The amount of bandit attacks had lessened considerably making us wonder if they were actually mercenaries Sorden hired to keep the fear in Shayd, so he would look like a hero to the people. We would never know for sure. The Capital was looking better and people changed their flags to that of the old compass crest. I knew it made Kip happy to see the symbol displayed again.

Oskai had sailed the rescued royals to Under. The Kings and Queen had gone home once they recuperated and helped eradicate skor from their respective kingdoms. Eventually they came back to Shayd to do an official crowning ceremony for Kip. Even though he was an heir of the original Shayd royal family, he had been gone so long that he felt it was necessary to be established and crowned by the other kingdoms. They completely supported the new King of Shayd which eased the transition for the people.

I had offered Cailyn a position as an elite warrior, but Shanm convinced her to join him in Farlo and last we heard, they were exploring both the Kingdom and each other. Tlaren became King shortly after his return to Tripscari but that did not stop him from visiting often and helping out Shayd in whatever way he could. Edrah and Edsen were closer than ever and often wrote to Kip and me as well as sent Drislian wood to help with rebuilding efforts.

Oskai had returned as quickly as possible once word of Sorden's death reached him and the other pirates had been slowly helping those in Under transition to the land above. Although those who wished to stay under the sea were allowed and a new council was put in place since Kip's original council came to live at the palace and took new positions as his advisors. We all lived in Skorval for now as construction was under way for a new castle in the Capital of Shayd, where Kip's old home used to be.

I had received mixed reactions from people both in reports and in person. Some believed me to be an extension of Sorden and therefore trying to take their free will and ruin the world. However, a much larger part of the population believed me to be a hero since stories had been told far and wide of my adventures with the pirates and love for the new King. I knew there would be those who did not like me which was another part of why I waited to marry Kip. I needed them to know I was a warrior and loyal citizen first.

Finally, after a few weeks, things began settle down and Kip was starting to get used to his new role. However, the one thing he wanted most was to go out to sea again, and that was why I found myself sitting in a small cabin facing a mirror as the room around me rocked side to side. Edrah and Jasta stood in there with me, Jasta braiding my hair into a circle around my head and Edrah applying makeup to my face. I was not wearing my red coat or my sheaths and swords. I felt bare without them but the white dress I had on instead was worth it.

"Ok, Ana, you are all ready."

"Wait, one more thing," Edrah said quickly.

We looked over to her as she grabbed a delicate silver circlet from a desk and placed it carefully on my head, nestling it in my braid circle. It was a gift from Kip. We decided to do a private wedding ceremony but a public crowning ceremony for me at a later date in which I would use the circlet again. By marrying

Kip, I was technically becoming Queen, but we felt the public ceremony later would be beneficial for the people in making it official.

It felt strange to wear it. I reached up and touched the metal but pulled my hand away, not wanting to disturb its placement.

They stepped back enough to let me stand and together we left the small cabin. Just before the stairs I stopped and turned back to the two women and smiled.

"This is it, yes?"

They grinned and nodded in unison.

"You will be a great Queen," Edrah said.

"And you get to be with the love of your life. What could be better?" Jasta added.

I sniffed, trying to hold in tears, and nodded.

They patted me on the back as I turned to the stairs. I took a deep breath and ascended, music instantly starting to play as I made my appearance. The two women behind me followed closely. The ship beneath us bobbed gently on the water and nothing was around except for the salty air and sea. Just as peaceful and joyous as we wanted.

I looked up and among the sails was a tan and green flag with the crest of Shayd on it. I remembered when Kip told me what it meant, and I suddenly felt the need to uphold its promise. The north pointed to the mountains where the heart of the kingdom was settled. The south pointed to the sea where our kingdom ended and began. Both signifying also that no part of Shayd would be ignored, from the sea to the mountains. The east was a sword promising the people they were protected, and the west was an eye to symbolize we were attentive and would watch out for them.

I brought my gaze back down to the waiting crowd. All of our friends, whether pirate, royal, or common citizen, were there on either side of an aisle made of rose petals. Kip had even invited the woman and her husband, Beatrice and Gino, who helped heal him after the fall. Despite the numerous people between me and the wooden alter covered in tropical flowers, I sought out the only one that mattered. Kip stood with his hands clasped in front of him, his blue coat billowing around him and instead of a tri-pointed hat, a gold crown sat prominently on his head. He looked like a mix between a Captain and a King, which meant he was all Kip.

I walked slowly down the aisle, each step taking me to my new life. Kip grinned at me and bounced on his feet in anticipation. His nervous and excited energy made me laugh and I had to hold in tears as joy threatened to burst out of me.

When I was close enough, Kip stepped forward and held out a hand. As soon as I took it, he pulled me toward him until I was standing in front of him and Jasta and Edrah parted to go join the other guests.

"By the stars and sea, you are beautiful." He looked me up and down, taking in every detail. His eyes lingered on my silver circlet before coming down to meet my eyes.

I blushed and he pulled me close until we were only a few inches apart.

We looked to our officiant who was shirtless in classic Tlaren style, but this time he sported two zigzag tattoos on his upper arm, indicating his kingly status. Tlaren grinned at us before launching into his speech about true love and his friendship with us both. His words faded as I gazed into Kip's eyes. It was almost hard to believe that we were there, in that moment, when only a couple months ago Kip had kidnapped me and convinced me to help him overthrow my uncle. I did not know it then but that first meeting with Kip would lead to the happiest moment of my life and I would not have it any other way. We continued to gaze at each other, each of us taking in every line and feature of the other. We responded when Ren prompted but otherwise were completely lost in one another.

"You may now kiss the bride," Ren eventually said, snapping me out of my thoughts.

"Ready?" Kip whispered, leaning in ever so slowly, love blazing in his eyes.

"With you by my side, I am ready for anything."

Then he kissed me.

"All hail, Queen Anameta! All hail, King Kipsien!"

The shouts rang around us, but it was only background noise to the love and happiness pounding in my chest.

My name is Anameta and I am a Queen

Kingdoms and Locations

Under

Rulers: Captain and the Council of Four

    Council of Four: Lenman, Oskai, Gesebe, Jasta

Resources: Anything they can steal, gadgets and inventions

Geography: A city in a glass dome underwater south of Shayd.

Flag: N/A

Skorval

Rulers: Lord Sorden

    Anameta heir to Skorval

Resources: Skor

Geography: Three mountains surrounding a valley in northeast Shayd

Flag: Three mountains with a crown above and three stars below surrounded by laurel leaves

Tripscari Islands

Rulers: King Trost

    Prince Tlaren heir to Tripscari

Resources: Fish, fruit, healing water

Geography: Four tropical islands make a circle around a larger fifth island.

Flag: divided into three quadrants with three tropical flowers in the top quadrant, two crossed spears in the left quadrant, and a waterfall in the right quadrant

Drisl

Rulers: Queen Emelda, King Darsen

      Prince Edsen

      Princess Edrah heir to Drisl

Resources: Wood, Drislian thread

Geography: Forest region with giant trees situated west of Farlo

Flag: A silver tree with purple swirls around it on a green background

Farlo

Rulers: King Domen, Queen Rala

      Prince Shanm heir to Farlo

      Prince Jiko, Princess Jaija

Resources: Glass, Wind harnessing technology

Geography: Desert region with sand dunes and caves situated in between Shayd and Drisl

Flag: A sun mandala over sand dunes on a black background

Shayd (Before the assassinations)

Rulers: King Karso, Queen Thali

    Prince Karstian heir to Shayd

    Prince Kipsien

Resources: Metal

Geography: Mountainous with some forested areas and beaches east of Farlo.

Flag: A compass with mountains in the north, an eye in the west, a sword in the east, and squiggly lines representing water in the south

Note from the Author

Ways to help Independent authors (without paying anything!):

--Rate and review the book on Amazon and Goodreads

--Follow them on social networks

--Post about the book

--Recommend to friends, family, and even strangers.

Your support means everything and would be much appreciated.

Acknowledgements

I want to give a big shout out to Chris and Con Designs because the original designer I used on the other two books in this series mysteriously vanished and I had to scramble to find someone else to finish the series off. I was so grateful to find Chris on 99Designs, who made an amazing cover and styled it to look like the other books. Not only that but he was quick to respond and easy to work with.

I also want to give thanks to Victoria Gillette, my #1 Beta Reader and cheer squad, not to mention motivational coach if constantly asking when the last book would be out counts as motivational coaching. I truly appreciate her help during the final stages of the book and her constant support.

About the Author

Katie Dunn grew up in the hot part of Arizona where she graduated NAU and became a teacher. She got a taste of the author life after her first YA contemporary fantasy novel Ancient Elements. Finding out she loved writing just as much as reading, teaching, and traveling, she sat down and wrote the first installment of the YA fantasy adventure Skor Stone trilogy: Pirates from Under and YA contemporary fantasy novel Myth Blessed. She has a notebook full of other ideas and will slowly be adding more stories to her author library.

You can check out more about Katie Dunn's books and works in progress at Kdunnauthor.com or Facebook.com/AuthorKatieDunn/